La Sagouine

Other books by Antonine Maillet in English Translation:

Novels

The Tale of Don l'Orignal, tr. by Barbara Goddard, Toronto: Clarke Irwin, 1978.

Pelagie —The Return to a Homeland, tr. by Philip Stratford, New York and Toronto: Doubleday, 1982.

The Devil Is Loose, tr. by Philip Stratford, Toronto: Lester & Orpen Dennys, 1986.

Mariaagélas, Maria, Daughter of Gélas, tr. by Ben-Z. Shek, Toronto: Simon & Pierre, 1986.

On the Eighth Day, tr. by Wayne Grady, Toronto: Lester & Orpen Dennys, 1989.

Plays

Evangeline the Second, tr. Luis de Céspedes, Toronto: Simon & Pierre, 1987.

Gapi and Sullivan, tr. Luis de Céspedes, Toronto: Simon & Pierre, 1987.

La Sagouine

Antonine Maillet

Translated by Luis de Céspedes

Simon & Pierre
Toronto, Canada

We would like to express our gratitude to the Canada Council and the Ontario Arts Council for their support.

Cover design by Jacques Léveillé from a sketch by Claude Gauvin

ISBN 0-88924-185-6

Second Edition, fourth printing
4 5 • 8 7 6 5

Canadian Cataloguing in Publication Data
Maillet, Antonine, 1929-
(La Sagouine, English)
La Sagouine
Translation of: La Sagouine

ISBN 0-88924-185-6
I. Title. II. Title: La Sagouine. English.

PS8526.A54S3413   1986   C843'.54   C86-093341-5
PQ3919.2.M26S3413   1986

General Editor: Marian M. Wilson

Printed and Bound in Canada

Order from
Simon & Pierre Publishing Co. Ltd.
2181 Queen Street East, Suite 301
Toronto, Ontario, Canada M4E 1E5

To my brother Achille
A.M.

CONTENTS

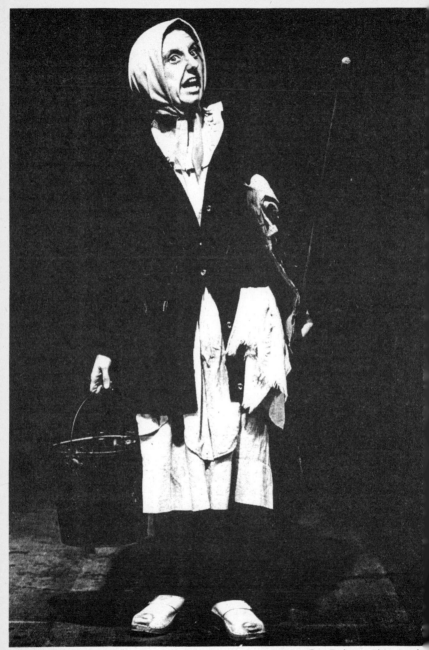

La Sagouine, a part
created by Viola Léger

Guy Dubois - Photograph
Montré...

FOREWORD

This is a true story. The story of La Sagouine, a scrubwoman, a woman of the sea, who was born with the century, with her feet in the water. Water was her fortune: the daughter of a cod fisherman, a sailor's girl, and later the wife of a fisherman who took oysters and smelts. A cleaning woman also, who ends up on all fours, with her bucket in front and her hands in the water.

That is where I found her, between her mop and her rags, bending over that pail of dirty water that has been collecting for half a century all the dirt of the country. Muddy water perhaps, but still capable of reflecting the face of a woman who can only see herself through other people's dirt.

I give her to you as she is, without touching up her wrinkles, her chapped hands, nor her language.

I

THE TRADE

Maybe I got a dirty face 'n cracked skin but, Mister, my hands are white! my hands are white 'cause I had 'em in water all my life. Spent my life cleanin. It don't mean I ain't in rags... I been cleanin fer others. Sure I look dirty, spent my life cleanin other people's dirt. Scrub 'n scrape 'n unstick chews of gum... they can have clean houses all right. Us, we ain't got no one to come 'n clean our place.

Ain't got no one to wash our clothes either. 'n sew 'n mend. They can sure say we're in rags: we wear the ol' coats they gave us fer the sake of Jesus Christ. Lucky they got some religion; makes 'em think sometimes 'bout givin us their ol' stuff... out of charity. Their ol' stuff 'n their ol' clothes that one day was new 'n that one day we use' to dream about. Course, by the time we get 'em as pay fer the work we done, we sure ain't dreamin about 'em any more.

When you've seen a velvet hat on a lady's head fer ten years, first you kind of like it, 'n you wanna have it. Then it starts gettin bumpy 'n ends up lookin like a buckwheat pancake. That's when they give it to you. And shawls they give you, when nobody wears 'em no more, 'n lace boots when shoes are in style. Sometimes they even give you two galoshes fer the same foot, or a coat too small... after they took the buttons off fr'm it. They sure can find we ain't dressed good all right.

We ain't dressed good 'nough fer church, better believe it! To go to church, that's when folks put on their best clothes. To go to church on Sunday. All of us, we ain't got not'n to wear fer a Sunday church. So, sometimes, we go on weekdays. But some folks jus' don't wanna go back no more, 'cause the priests tol'em a weekday mass don't count. The're jus' sinnin so'more when they get Holy Communion on Friday with Sunday's mass on their conscience. When Gapi saw that, he stopped goin on Fridays and Sundays, so we ain't goin a lot these days.

And fer St. Blaise's day, we ain't havin our throats blessed either, 'cause we gotta stay 'n keep house fer'em while they go to church, so, what happens is all year long our tonsils get a beating, to say not'n of the mumps. The others that got their throats blessed all they can, they feel good 'n they look down on us 'n our flu. Well now, flus is like all sicknesses: never 'nough to go around, 'n they always catch the same people. Funny how we're always at the end of the line fer everything else, but fer flus 'n fer lice, ah! well...

They don't wanna have our kids in front of the class, near the others, cause their heads is full of lice, 'n those that never got 'em are more afraid of lice 'n fleas than cancer. Mus' think they can eat a man alive. They don't mind stuffin a pound of shoe polish or bear fat on their own mop of hair, but if they see a louse as big as a herrin's egg on somebody else's hair... Don't wanna sit beside our kids 'n they send 'em to the back of the class where they don't see 'n und'stand not'n. Ain't easy to get some education when you can't see the blackboard 'n you can't hear the school-teacher.

Ain't easy either to learn to talk high-class 'n act civilized with civilized folks, when you ain't allowed to talk to 'em without lookin saucy. Jus' you go 'n say: hi-ya! to Dominique's missus, while gettin in through the front door to wash her floor. She'll pinch her nose like if your hi-ya! didn' smell good. So when the next time comes aroun', you get in through the back door 'n you shut yer mouth.

Ain't easy to know what to say to those folks. Them, well, they can talk 'bout their kin, their trips to the ol' countries, their summer houses 'n their winter houses, 'n they can talk 'bout their kids bein in college or in the gove'ment. But us, we ain't got no educated boys, no kin'folk in the States, 'n we can't change houses fr'm one season to the other, or go to som'other country, lik'em tourists. We ain't got no holidays cause we ain't got no jobs. We work aroun' the houses. 'n they ain't no paid holidays there. No forty-hour week either, 'n no pension fer yer ol' days. Yer ol' days, you spend 'em like the other days: scrapin 'n cleanin... Yep!...

And yet, we sure wouldn' of minded to have us our ol' years well planted in good earth, 'n well cared fer. The kind of years you get in time of plenty, like they says. Ah! ain't talkin of those trips with the senior critizens' crowd, you can't set yer hopes too high. Cause the're those that spend their ol' age jus' like that, they says, wanderin fr'm town to town, 'n fr'm country to country, on big trailers that look so much lik'a house, you can't tell the difference, they says. Well, those that can afford in their ol' age a house that runs on four wheels, along the big highways, they must of got one that was well anchored on a good basement, when they was young.

And that's som'n Gapi never und'stood. Now, jus' you tell me, he says, what can a person want, goin that far, when you got all you need at home? When you eat yer three meals a day at yer table; 'n you sleep yer whole nights on a spring-mattress; 'n come Fall, you change fr'm changin yer summer underwear to changin yer winter underwear; 'n you got yer front porch, 'n rockin chair that rocks so far back you can see all aroun' you, 'n far into the bay, 'n... Ah! Gapi, it takes a lot to make him happy, that one.

But sometimes I say to him: maybe a person that got all that, 'n that saw so far ahead of him, maybe he can't stop fr'm wannin to see s'more 'n to see farther. So that's when he joins the senior citizens, 'n gets 'mself a trailer, 'n takes to the road.

I dunno, but seems to me that it can't be too unpleasant to leave like that fer the ol' countries, one mornin, jus' to go 'n see, to poke yer nose aroun', without havin to do not'n. Seems to me mus' be nice to go 'n see what you ain't seen before, like the Niagara Falls, 'r the soldier with the plaid skirt that plays the bagpipes in Nova Scotia. Seems to me that I'd like to see that, one day, fer no reason, jus' to see.

And havin gone that far, I sure woudn' of minded goin back to the land of my forefathers, to Prince Edward Island that is, to see if it changed much in the last hundred years. Ah! not to stay 'n to set up my home, jus' to look at the country, 'n the folks, 'n to see if it's true the gardens down there grow faster than the ones 'round here. 'n try to find the kin'folk that stayed there after the Expulsion. They says that in the ol' coutries, you don't need to give yer name: you can tell the Thibodeau's by their eyes; 'n the Leblanc's by their nose; 'n the Bourgeois' cause of the dimple in their chin; 'n the Goguen's cause of the way they pr'nounce their r's, like they had an orange stuck in the throat.

Yep, kin'folk fr'm the folks down here that you find down there. Be real nice to get us all t'gether one day; 'n to reco'nize each other; 'n slap on an ol' man's shoulder 'n call him by his first name; 'n greet the offsprin of yer great-great-grandfather *Pit à Boy à Thomas Picoté*, 'n find fr'm a distance a person that looks like you, 'n speaks yer language, 'n does yer same work, 'n wouldn' look down on you cause yer not'n but a scrubwoman that ain't never done not'n 'n never seen not'n.

Nope, never seen not'n but somebody else's floor that I go 'n clean each day the Good Lord brings. Their hardwood floors 'n flowery tiling where you get on yer knees like when you pray. And you scrub. You scrub 'n collect their dirt that you bring back at night in yer bucket. Everybody else's dirt in the bottom of yer bucket... That's the way it goes!...

This is the dirtiest place I ever cleaned... Even chewing-gum you got, on a nice oilcloth like this; don't make no sense. Holy Mother of Christ, some people just ain't got no pride. Jus' you give a new oilcloth to *la Sagouine*, let me tell you she'll put her gum in her spittoon. Her gum 'n her tobacco. Each thing in its place, I tell you, and a place fer each thing. Well here, there's no spittoon... they pr'tend it ain't done no more. So they drop their gum on the floor, 'n their ashes everywhere. Everywhere on the tables, the arm-chairs, the carpets, or scattered all over the place, in small ashtrays the size of my bellybutton. A nice, big spittoon right in

the middle of the floor 'd save you fr'm the trouble
of pickin up the ashes 'n scrapin the chewing-gum
everywhere.

They say it ain't so messy 'cause to smoke, they
pucker their lips, like this... Don't wanna hear not'n
about chewing tobacco, makes 'em feel sick. To
chew tobacco maybe makes more spit, but a lot less
smoke. And it ain't spit that bothers, but smoke
'cause you can't shove smoke in a spittoon. Sure
makes me heave to think each time you breathe in
you inhale everybody's smoke.

And some of those folks get sick too, you know,
even them that have their skins real white 'n shiny.
They got nice skin, 'n curly hair all over their head,
'n nails as long as this 'n as sharp as a steeple. 'n
they smell of lotion 'n toothpaste like you wanna
faint. Looks real clean fr'm the outside. But fr'm the
inside? Ain't no one to know what's crawling inside
if you ain't seen it fer yerself. I know they can
operate now so they can see it all. An open belly,
an open heart, an open head... yep, they even open
yer head nowadays, better believe it! I heard you
can get yer head split way down to yer neck. They
ain't gonna see *la Sagouine* flat on her back in an
operation room, 'n gettin her body open' to see
what's in her head... 'n what's in her head, she
ain't been hiding anyway. Gapi says if you hide
yerselves 'n watch what the doctors can find in their
patients' bodies, you sure ain't gonna find a Christmas dinner in there. You never know. I figure an
open body mus' look like any other open body. It's
when the're closed up again, with their skin real tight
'round the neck 'n 'round the stomach, that a rich
man's body don't look like a poor man's body no
more. Anyway, most of the sicknesses of the rich

folks come fr'm their nerves. And a nerve sickness don't show. They got their little breakdowns fr'm time to time, but they ain't cross-eyed, 'n they ain't got blacken' skin, 'n boils in the face, 'n twisted joints, 'n water knees. That's what screws up a person. But breakdowns... all the rich folks hav'em, 'n they can hav'em with their nice clothes on their backs, 'n it don't show none. I says this to Gapi: you get rich sickness 'n you get poor sickness, 'n it ain't the same sickness. Each thing in its place, like he says...

...Ain't easy to be poor. Some people think only the rich folks got troubles. The rich folks, they got troubles in their heart 'n in their head. But us, we got our troubles in our bones. Yep... comes a time when a person 's got not'n but his bones. 'n that day, it's in yer bones yer troubles go. Doctors call 'em rhumatism, arthrism 'r som'n like that. They gotta giv 'em names, if the're doctors. 'n they also give you a little bottle of liniment to rub yer back. You can rub yer back with all the ads in the Almanac, you ain't gonna get rid of the pain in yer bones. Too much cold you got stored up in there. 'n too much lumbago 'n shingles. When all yer life you've been bending down to scrub floors, you can rub yer back with liniment all you want, you'll end up broken down. Ain't that easy to straighten up when you're poor. And besides, you never use' to walk with yer head high, when you was young.

...When you was young 'n when you was old. Poor people are made to drag their clogs fr'm pavement to pavement, 'n door to door. Drag yer clogs, yer rag 'n yer bucket. You'll leave yer clogs on the porch so you won't mess up the floor you're gonna clean up: you'll supply yer own mop, 'n yer pail 'n yer soap; you'll kneel down on a piece of cardboard so you ain't gettin water on yer knees; you'll take on large stretches of floor to show 'em you don't mind hard work; you'll scrape the gum with a blade, 'n you'll make the nail-heads shine; you'll scrub, rinse, clean... 'n at night, they'll give you yer pay 'n some ol' clothes they don't wanna wear no more. You'll get out of there with yer skin a little more cracked, 'n yer bones a shade stiffer, but Mister, you'll have yer hands white!

...God almighty, yes! All the women 'round here can wash their skin in buttermilk 'n lotion all they want, but they ain't never gonna be able to have whiter hands than *la Sagouine*, that spent her life with her hands in water.

II

_____ YOUTH

Ah! I was young when I was young, yep, me too, young 'n beautiful, like the others. Well that's what they use' to say. 'n when I looked at myself in the mirror — had a hand mirror in 'em days — I didn' make me sick... Ah, no sir, seems I didn' make nobody sick in my time. 'n then, time ends up passin, 'n you along with it. But while it lasts, youth is the best of times. That's fer sure, the best of times.

Today's youth ain't like that. It grumbles, kicks'n looks down on everythin. It don't know what it wants. Us, we knew. We knew just about exactly what we wanned; real easy, we wanned everythin. Couldn' have it all, but we wanned as much as possible. Ah! we wasn' folks to be happy with only the smaller half. Nope, nope, nope!... no half-a-pancake, 'r half-a-shack, 'n no half-a-man either. Nope, youth ain't a time fer halves. Like the priest says, it's a time fer great ideals. Well, I had'em, ideals of my own.

...I was young 'n good-lookin. Had all my teeth 'n all my hair. 'n smooth skin too, 'n sharp finger-nails. I was... yep... ah! didn' make nobody sick. So the day I figured that out, well, had no need to think it over too much to find'em ideals of mine. Comes real easy, an ideal. You lean on a telephone pole near Arvin's, 'r on the edge of the wharf, 'n you can be sure they'll be comin fr'm all over, each one as ideal as the other. 'n then, you're stuck on havin to make a choice. Even if you want everythin, you can't have it all at once. It's like Dominique's missus says, her boy couldn' become a priest, a doctor 'n a lawyer. Ain't easy to choose between'em, so he got'mself into politics. But me couldn' very well pick politics... Heh!... after all, I was only a woman, 'n a low-class one at that... A low-class woman, she just about has one choice only. But that choice, well, she don't make it half way. We got no vocation, but ideals we sure have. A low-class girl that's still nice 'n plump, 'n young lookin, well it so happens that if she's got a head on her shoulders, she can take her pick. One at a time, that is.

You lean on the telephone pole... 'r you walk up 'n down the Post Road, fr'm *La Butte du Moulin* to *La Rivière à Hache*, 'n you watch. Well, don't lose heart, won't be long you ain't gonna be watchin no more cause it's them others that'll be watchin you. 'n then, don't show'em you noticed, keep on chewin yer gum 'n watchin the water flow under the bridge, but don't let'em out of yer sight. You'll be seein *Gilbert à François à Etchenne* straightenin up 'n runnin his fingers through his hair, as well as the widow's boy hidin behind his swing, 'r big *Pacifique* 'mself peepin' out of the curtains. Heh!... well, you won't let'em catch you behind curtains, you ain't that crazy. *Sagouine* 'r no *Sagouine*, you gotta respect yerself!...

You won't be able to respect yerself fer long, cause you gotta live... So, you adjus' yer ideals to yer means. You chew two pieces of gum, you put a touch of perfume on yer neck 'n behind yer ears 'n you stretch yer walk all the way to the *Ruisseau des Pottes*. There, you can be sure the'll always be people aroun'. The'll be people, but the'll also be *la Bessoune.* 'n if you get too close to the cape, the'll be *la Sainte.* Ah! that one, she sure's got a way. She catches'em all with rosaries 'n medais. Even *Basile à Pierre*, she got'm to join her in thirty-three ways of the cross. What they was doin in between'em ways of the cross, that, no one can say fer sure... Well, schooners 'n steamers will always be comin. Like I always says, as long as there's a wharf somewhere... The sea, that's what saved us all. Without smelts, clams, oysters 'n sailors...

Came fr'm all over, 'em sailors. A lotta times, couldn' catch a word that came out of their noses. Wasn' people fr'm aroun' here, but they was good folks nevertheless. Gapi, he always says you gotta watch out. Well, he ain't got trust too close to his heart, Gapi. 'n yet, when the war was declared, — the last one, that is, — they was a big steamer alongside the wharf that hadn' seen it comin 'n didn' have time to get out of the bay. Full of Germans, in there, folks that wasn' on our side. They grabbed'em 'n shoved'em in jail. Some says it was a good thing, that you can't let the bad guys go runnin around' hurtin folks. 'n yet, do we know on what side is the good folks? 'n is all the good folks on the same side? Sure upsettin, that is. A girl can try 'n sleep on her good side all she wants at night, but she can't help thinkin she met a couple of sailors that seemed real nice, even if they was on the wrong side.

I remember the one that use' to mumble a couple of words of English, even if he wasn' fr'm England 'r the States, 'n English wasn' his mother tongue either. Nope, he spoke a weird language that sounded like not'n you ever heard. Well, to make 'mself und'stood, he'd picked up a little English in the isles, so we managed talkin to each other.

Course, with the others, I wasn' in the habit of talkin much, 'r fer that matter, we really didn' try to und'stand each other. But that one...

He had blond hair, 'n sad eyes. Took me a long while to know why. The sad eyes, I mean. Actually, I can say I never really knew the whole story. Didn' know much, to tell you the truth. Jus that som'n must of happened to him in his far away country. Cause he was always singin the same ol' song 'bout the deportation of a family. That's what he explained to me. Never laughed, that one, 'n he didn' seem to enjoy life like the others. That's how come nobody wanned to have him, not even the girls fr' m *la Butte-du-Moulin*. But me...

At first, I sort of felt sorry fer him, 'n a kind of compassion. Skinny, he was, 'n always singin by 'mself, sittin on the bow. So, I'd get real close to him, 'n I'd sit by his side 'n keep quiet. We would both be lookin far into the sea. Bit by bit, he started singin while I was there, 'n lookin at me also; 'n at the end, we was talkin to each other 'n murderin the English language, like they says. 'n that's when I started noticin his sad eyes 'n his thick mop of blond hair, 'n his hands whiter 'n better kept than that of a lawyer, better believe it. 'n when he sang, it would make my insides churn like someone had punched me in the stomach. Didn' und'stand why, but I didn' notice the others no more, 'n even turned down good propositions. Gapi 'mself realized that...

Ah! wasn' easy, wasn' easy to explain. Seemed to me the sea had changed colour. It was a deeper blue than usual, 'n the fish was swimmin near the surface of the water like they wanned to play with the seagulls. The others started teasin us, 'n callin

us names, but it didn' bother me none... almos'
none...

...Then, one day, at sunrise, they declared war.
'n the steamer was caught inside the bay; 'n they
shoved the sailors in prison fer the whole time of the
war, they says, cause they was on the wrong side.
That's how come you hadda kill'em 'n shov'em in
prison. Right then'n there, seems the sea changed
colour, 'n even the seagulls never cried like they
did before. You can try all you want to fall asleep at
night... but you worry, 'n you can't help wonderin.

...Then, they comes a time when you wonder
so'more cause you're no longer as young as you
use' to be. That kind of thinkin comes with the
years. Maybe it's cause when you get older, you got
more time to think... Ain't easy to know fer sure.
Gapi, he says thinkin is only good to give yerself
ulcers in the stomach. Well, Gapi sure mus' have his
stomach covered with'em, cause he never did not'n
else in his life apart fr'm bein grouchy.

...There's only one thing wrong with Gapi: he's
an ol' grouch and he always was. Why, he use'to
take a fit each time I was goin to town, cause Gapi,
he wasn' use' to it. At first, I didn' have to exile
myself to get by. Could stay in these parts; they was
enough work between le Ruisseau des Pottes 'n
la Butte du Moulin. But when you start gettin older,
bit by bit you gotta let go some territory, cause
you ain't the only one to make a livin. 'n when you're
no longer young, you can bet there's folks younger
than you aroun'. 'n at the end, you can chew yer
three pieces of gum fer all you're worth, 'n wear out
the gravel of the Post Road, you won't even catch a
glimpse of Gilbert à François à Etchenne, not even

a shadow of *Pacifique* behind his curtains. So, you gotta exile yerself. 'n you take the bus, 'n once a week, you go in town. Gapi could never hack it, cause here at least, he saw what was goin on. But in town... Come then, I tol'm, come 'n see fer yerself... Not a chance. He gripes, but he don't move... Ain't easy...

'n then, there's your kids that start gettin older. That's the way it goes, can't help that. Then, once they've grown, well they got eyes as big as saucers, 'n they ask you questions. If you're goin to scrub the floor of the station, how come you don't take along yer bucket 'n yer mop?... So you end up takin with you yer bucket 'n yer mop, cause you really end up on the floor of the station. Yep... when they ain't no more work on Main Street, you wind up cleanin the floor of the station. 'n the one of *l'Assomption*, 'n the one of Radio-Canada. Ah! when you're down on all fours on the floor of Radio-Canada... yer down pretty low... pretty low, cause it's fr'm down there, with yer hands in yer bucket 'n yer nose in yer rag, that you see on the floor the reflection of faces you know... yep... In'em buildin's, you got a lot of people passin through in one day, 'n there's always some men passin by that you already saw on that Main Street of yers. Them, they don't reco'nize you, but you sure reco'nize'em. 'n you ask yerself when is it yer at yer lowest: with yer knees on your bucket 'r... A person's gotta live, you see. It's the only thing that counts. Ideal 'r no ideal, comes a time when a person's gotta live 'n make ends meet.

...As long as between'em two ends, you don't catch somethin else. That's the biggest misfortune. You get use' to everythin, bit by bit: you let'em

catch you, 'n drop you, 'n catch you again, 'n
drop you again, 'n you know you're gonna lose yer
telephone pole 'n end up on the floor of the station.
You get use' to that without complainin, it's yer job.
But why is it you gotta catch all sorts of things on
top of that? Remember *la belle Adélaïde*, the
daughter à *Philippe au P'tit Jean*? If ever in this
country there was a beautiful creature, it was her.
Plump 'n red, 'n sly like nobody else. But she sure
wasn' easy to handle. Like they says, she had licen-
tiousness 'n roguery in her blood. She wasn' an
offspring of the *Bois-Francs de Memramcook* fer
not'n. Well, do you wanna know? She hadn' stood
three years by that pole of hers, that her legs was
swollen like barrels, 'n she had pimples all over
her arms 'n cheeks. After three years, she wasn' fit to
look at, the poor soul. If you think that's fair! Gapi,
he says that it was good fer her, that she had it
comin... But Gapi, he don't know what he's talkin
about. Jus' has to be an ol' grouch.

     The worst was when a big ship arrived fr'm the
ol' countries 'n you thought they was gonna be lots
of work aroun', but at the same time you had all of
them girls fr'm the surroundin hills that would come
jumpin down like an Egyptian plague of locusts.
All the way fr'm the back-country they came. 'n
worst than flies they was. 'n don't you worry, they
would take over the place. Even if 'em nights you
was out by six o'clock, you could be sure fr'm
the start that all the poles was taken. The poles 'n
the bridge. You could even see some of them waitin
on the steps of the church, imagine that! Don't got
no style, them people, 'n no respect at all. Ain't got
no manners 'n they come here takin over our places.
You should of seen 'em with all that flour on their
face 'n beet juice on their cheeks! If they ever was

people that knew all about beet juice 'n flour, it was us. Couldn' show us how it works. They looked like any ol' thing you could imagine, 'n they was tryin to take away yer livin. They wasn' happy with chewin any ordinary gum either, 'r wood gum; had to be the kind that made bubbles, 'n they would burst'em right under yer nose to show off. But there came a time when we had it just about up to here with their bubble gum, 'n their puckered lips, 'n their flour-powdered noses. 'n all of them fatter than floaters, on top of that, two-yolk girls, we use' to call'em. But'em two-yolk girls had a yolk too many, cause they took everythin away fr'm us: our poles, our Post Road, our livin. 'n that's how come we had to leave fer the city, jus' like the Holy Family... When a person 's no longer young, ain't easy... ain't easy at all.

...It's never easy when a person's gotta make a livin. Ah! fer that matter, we ain't alone. Everybody's gotta earn a livin. The doctors, 'n the insurance salesmen, 'n the people fr'm the gov'ment, they work as hard as we do. Like us, the're always on the road, night 'n day. 'n they gotta be nice to people, 'n they gotta promise more than they can give, 'n they gotta... they gotta stoop real low sometimes. Them also, it ain't always clean the work they do. Seems you got some doctors that give birth to two pairs of twins a night; 'n agronomists that studied fer years in colleges 'n end up shovin their noses in manure to see if it's good; 'n lawyers, 'n members of gov'ment... them ones, if I could tell you what they have to do to earn a livin... We ain't the only ones that gotta work hard, 'n we ain't complainin. After all, some folks is worst off than us. I always says it: when you're bent on complainin, *la Sagouine*, look aroun' you; you'll realize that life is tough fer everyone, 'n there's always some folks that is worse off than you...

Comes a time when that's what makes you feel better, knowin you ain't alone.

III

_____ **CHRISTMAS**

I may be *une Sagouine*, sure, but I know what a christian Christmas is all about. Saw seventy-two of them in my short life, ain't that 'nough to get the picture? Specially since they all look alike, their Christmasses. All the same, they is. Bells, stars, toys, crepe paper, angels, Santas 'n a manger beside the sanctuary. A nice manger, made of thick brown paper that limitates stone like you couldn' tell the difference, jus' like I'm tellin you. 'n animals all aroun' to fill the gaps: sheep, camels, shepherds, 'n a good half-dozen wise men carryin gifts: gold, fur 'n incense... never und'stood how you could give incense to a new-born baby fer a present. Don't make sense to me, but seems like it's written down, 'n we sure ain't gonna start gripin'bout the Bible at a time like this.

But at our place, Christmas didn' start in church; started at Arvin's. Goes to say that, in my time, we didn' need the calendar of *l'Aratouère* to see Christmas comin; we jus' had to watch'em Arvin's windows. Then, one day, they'd all start lightin up, 'em shop-windows. Was all limitation: the cakes, the angels, the donuts, 'n even the spruce wasn' real. Not that you can't find spruces in'em woods, it's jus' that a plastic spruce, like this, looks nicer, they says, 'n more expensive. Ah! fer that matter, when it came to Christmas spendin, at Arvin's they wasn' close-fisted. They had 'emselves a load of toys 'n clothes that'd make yer mouth water, jus' like I'm tellin you!

Wasn' like we could afford'em things, but we could watch. We'd see Dominique's missus that 'd jus' bought Christmas ornaments, 'n candles, 'n silver paper to decorate her tree; 'n the banker's children buyin peanuts by the pound 'n bananas too; 'n big *Carmélice*, the wife of *P'tit Georges*, that every year 'd buy 'erself a five pound box of Moirstri-X; 'n those that would buy teddy bears, 'n cryin dolls, 'n electric cars. Some children had it all fer Christmas 'n they would eat 'nough oranges to screw up their guts.

But the nearer you was to the Holiday Season, the more you had folks fr'm the back-country aroun'. Real savages, they was, you can take my word fer it that ain't never lied. They jus' had to see everythin, 'n they had to touch it all, worse than the folks of *Cocagne*, they was, I'm tellin you. Stand aside a bit, we'd tell'em. But no way. Them bums 'd take all the room, 'n if we would of let 'em, they would of taken away our Christmas.

So, we'd let'em have their shop-windows 'n we'd go to the bingo. Oh! not to play, we wasn' the kind of people that could afford buyin a card fer every bingo. But we'd go 'n watch the others play. Every Saturday night 'n sometimes on Sunday afternoons, the Ladies of St. Anne'd organize a church bingo fer the poor. So us, we'd go 'n look at'em play. Not fer long, cause to keep it orderly, they'd have some of them Sacred Heart League bouncers, 'n we'd always end up bein kicked out. All cause of *la Sainte* that never managed to keep her mouth shut 'n would always cry out at the barber's missus, tellin her where to put down her chips... Well anyway, we'd manage to catch a piece of the action.

We rarely missed the play either. Each year, the sisters pr'pared a Christmas play with the convent girls. They didn' charge not'n 'n they also had a door prize. Changed prizes every year, they did. *Boy à Polyte* came out with a statue of the Little Flower, *Francis Motté* got 'mself one of Mary Queen-o'-Hearts, 'n *La Cruche* won a Maria Goretti that was so big, she had to leave it in the convent chapel. Not everyone could win a statue, but we could sure watch the play. 'n we knew jus' when we hadda cry or sniff, cause we use' to see the play every year. A real nice play, gotta giv' em that. At the end of it, they was an angel with pink wings 'n a star on the forehead that would raise both arms 'n yell: "He came among us to save the poor!" 'n then, you hadda clear out real fast cause the nuns started openin the windows of the hall to bring in some fresh air.

On Christmas eve, they was also a handin out of presents in the church basement. All of the poor folks had a present comin to 'em. The kids, that is. When you started gettin older, you no longer had it comin; so we'd watch the hand-out. Seems it was the Eucharistic Crusaders that'd done all the wrappin, with the choir-boys. Each Advent, they'd work at pickin up all kinds of toys fr'm door to door 'n fixin them up, caus'em high-class kids wasn' gonna give away their good stuff to the poor ones. So then, on distribution day, they was a little sermon given by the priest that would always end by: "Love one another!" 'n all hell would break loose. You see, the kids that got an airplane that don't fly no more or else a little pissin doll that ain't pissin, well, they'd all start cryin 'n it would end up in a fight. Specially when they'd seen'em fer a whole month behind Arvin's windows, them flyin airplanes 'n pissin-dolls;

they knew their stuff. They got no gifts at home, but
they knew all about'em. So the choir-boys 'n the
Eucharistic Crusaders was all sad cause they'd done
all they could to come up with their good deed. But
the priest would tell'em, makes no sense bein sad
cause it's the tension that counts. So the choir-boys
would go back with their good deeds 'n the kids fr'm
below with their broken planes. 'n the followin day,
it was Christmas.

The real Christmas, not the Arvin's one, but the
one of the Christians, started in the twilight of the
night before. When the Liquor Store closed its doors,
everybody had to go home. So then, when all the
houses was lightin up, the town itself started lookin
like a big Christmas tree. Was the time of day we
usually had to slap the kids to send'em to bed,
but on that p'ticular night, you had to slap 'em to
keep'em on their feet. Yep! it's the only night of
the year 'em kids wanned to go to bed, cause of
Santa Claus that came down the chimney when they
was asleep. That was the other folks' kids that put'em
ideas in their heads, 'n they believed them. We
could talk til we was blue in the face tryin to make'em
und'stand Santa Claus jus' couldn' know where we
was livin, 'n we didn' even have a chimmey to begin
with... they didn' wanna und'stand not'n, 'em kids,
'n they'd fall asleep in our arms.

But they'd wake up when Noume started crankin
up his gramophone. Everybody 'd get together at
l'Orignal's place 'n there, Noume 'd bring out his
gramophone that he'd brought fr'm overseas. Some
tried to say Noume's gramophone wasn' given to
him. But'em ones had to deal with l'Orignal that
sweared he'd giv'em som'n to remember, if they
didn' shut up. So, we'd bring out the records 'n start

crankin up: Willy Lamotte, la Bolduc, 'n "It's a Long Way to Tipperary."

By eleven o'clock, 'em ones that could still stand up, 'd go to church fer the midnight mass. We'd leave early to try 'n find some room. Not to sit down, fer sure, us we didn' have no pew, but we had the right to be standin by the back of the center aisle, since it was Christmas. Couldn' really hear the mass cause they was no room fer us in the pews, but we could see the pr'cession when it was passin by the back of the church. The priest 'd put on his best clothes: cossacks, stoles, chasubles, 'n surplus over surplus like they was no tomorrow. 'n all of that in nun's lace. Then came the young priests, 'n the Children of Mary, 'n the choir-boys carryin a Child-Jesus-in-Wax, on a stretcher. They'd carry him with his beatiful face 'n his nice curly hair straight to the stable, between the mare 'n the ox.

Had no need to be afraid fer his white gown, that baby, didn' smell like a stable in there, they was no manure in his crib, better believe *la Sagouine*. Ah! nope. A beautiful manger it was, made of nice clean cardboard, with a nice blue silk blanket fer its crib, 'n good straw made of fine paper, 'n plush animals well trimmed... didn' stink like sheep 'r have a barn smell in there. We was the only ones that didn' smell good in the whole church, that's how come we stayed in the back. Didn' have no frilly clothes, none of us, 'n no curly hair. We wouldn' of dared to stand even beside the shepherds, better believe it!

Usually, we'd leave the church when the sermon started. It ain't that the priest didn' preach good... He had a voice you could of heard all the

way fr'm *le Fond de la Baie*, if he'd taken the trouble.
It's jus' that fer midnight mass, he would never raise
his voice, but whispered almost only fer the front
pews, cause he was moved. But us, we didn' und'stand
not'n. 'n we also didn' wanna come out same time
the others did, so we wouldn' be noticed. Then,
once "O Holy Night" 'n "O Little Town o' Bethle-
hem" was through, we'd all get together outside the
church door, 'n we'd go finish our Christmas at
home, in our shacks.

'n there, the manure was fer real, I'm tellin you,
'n so was the straw. 'n if we would of had a fallin
star to hook on our door frame, maybe the three
Wise Men would of made a mistake 'n carried
their gold 'n their incense in our homes. But they
never came... no one. So, Christmas turned out to
be like Arvin's or bingo: we wasn' buyin, we wasn'
playin, but we watched the others buy 'n play.
That's how come we saw the Child-Jesus-in-Wax
passin by 'n goin straight to his crib... 'n us, we went
straight home, like always.

Jus' suppose that on a Christmas day, the
pr'cession made a wrong turn 'n landed right here in
our shacks... the shepherds, the Wise Men, the
camels, Joseph 'n Mary, 'n the baby... The whole
Holy Family with the angels 'n the archangels, the
mare'n the ox, all of them losin their way 'n landin
home by chance... Can you imagine!

It'd be *Elisabeth à Zacharie* that would come
down fr'm the hills of *Sainte-Marie* to tell us one of
her cousins is expectin, now. 'n us, we'd hurry 'n
clean up the house, 'n find a cradle in *la Sainte's*
attic, 'n cut fer him a blanket in an ol' comforter;
'n we'd have everythin ready, all ready to welcome

him. 'n we'd wait. We'd wait fer the angels to start singin their Gloria in Excelsis Deo over the bay, warnin the others that a Child-was-born-to-you in one of the shacks by the waterfront.

'n then, we'd see the fishermen comin out of their fishin cabins, 'n all the poor folks leavin their shacks, 'n *la Sainte*, 'n *l'Orignal*, 'n *la Cruche*, 'n me 'n Gapi... 'n we'd send fer *Sarah Bidoche*, the midwife, to help jus' in case. But he wouldn' need *Sarah's* help, that little one, cause it would all happen accordin to the Bible, like a miracle. We'd get there right on time to see it all: the Child-Jesus in his mother's arms, with Joseph the presumptuous father, like they says, hangin on to his lily; 'n the mare 'n the ox puffin over the cradle to keep'm warm. 'n the Wise Men kneelin in front of him holdin presents. Real presents, this time aroun', no gold 'n no incense, but gifts fer a child, like a teddy bear 'r a spinnin-top that plays Christmas tunes.

At home, in our shacks, seems to me we wouldn' be ashamed of standin' by the shepherds 'n the camels. I'm sure *Don l'Orignal* would find som'n to say to Joseph 'n to the Wise Men. Maybe even Gapi would also mix with the men 'n give some of his tobacco to *Zacharie*. Yep, I really think so: *Zacharie* looks to me like a man pretty much like Gapi; he don't put his trust in people; 'n you can't make'm believe any ol'thing. Gapi 'd feel real good, sittin on the same bench as him.

I can jus' imagine *la Cruche* whisperin to the Holy Virgin, so she could tell her everythin, tell her everythin she never would of told the priest, that's fer sure. Or, maybe she'd say not'n at all, but would jus' stay close to her, 'n they'd laugh together, the two of them watchin the baby.

Then we'd send fer Noume with his gramo-
phone 'n his records, 'n *Gérard à Jos*, with his kazoo.
'n maybe we could sing him a ballad 'r "It's a Long
Way to Tipperary."

Course, *la Sainte* would jus' have to interfere
again 'n foul up the party. 'n she might very well
give a sermon to the whole Holy Family, 'n tell the
Wise Men to stand on each side of the cradle, 'n the
shepherds to keep their backs straight 'n one knee on
the ground. Pretty sure it ain't like that she would
of figured Christmas, *la Sainte*.

Ah! 'n I think she'd probably be right, too. If
the pr'cession lost its way 'n landed right in our
shacks... wouldn' be Christmas at all, no more.
Cause we sure wouldn' be able to decorate our
front-doors with crepe paper 'n colour lights, 'n we
got no bells either, no stars, no toys, no Santa Claus,
no manger made of thick brown paper to limitate
stone like you can't tell the difference. Nope, we'd
have not'n to welcome him, that Child-Jesus, no
lace, no silk blanket, no fine paper fer the straw.
Not'n at all to fix'm up a nice Nativity.

Nope, a nice Christmas like that jus'ain't made
fer poor folks.

IV

_____ THE GOOD NEW YEAR

Yep!... a real good year it was... a person can't complain... a real good year. It's me, *la Sagouine*, that's tellin you. Ain't had one like that since the famous rain-storm when a mean twister tore away the roofs of all the houses... A real good year. No snow cavin in, no sudden deaths, no maimed folks, no newmonia, no flooded basement... just a little bit... a few feet... anyway, don't bother me none, ain't got no basement... 'n no cold spell of below-zero weather, shiverin behind the stove. True, no blue-berries either... but so many haws 'n beechnuts, the squirrels would croak of indigestion. 'n clams real fat 'n full of mud, 'n weddins, a picnic at *Sainte-Marie*'s 'n elections... A damn good year, yep!

The good year of the poor folks, it was. You see, with a winter of mild weather, a summer of clams 'n a Fall of elections, what else can we ask fer? Take a good long cold winter fer instance, when a person's in real need of warmin up. Well, if we get cold weather, we have ice; 'n if we have ice on the bay, we can cross over it on a small sleigh to a cove where we gather kindlins 'n twigs to keep us warm. That year, we had a mild winter, no ice, but no cold either; no kindlins, but no need to keep yer stove white-hot 'n sit on it too... It works out pretty well, that way, 'n I gotta sayin of my own: there's a Good Lord meant jus' fer the poor folks... Gapi, he says we'd be better off with heat in the house, 'n ice over the bay. But he asks fer too much,

Gapi, that's what I says to him. Gotta take what the Good Lord gives us. 'n a person can't have it all.

Ah! fer that matter, some folks ain't too happy. They got to thinkin if the bay don't freeze, the fishermen ain't gonna be able to pull their shacks over the ice 'n the smelts are gonna stay under water. True, smelts are made to live under water... but us, we're made to eat if we wanna live. That's how come all year, you got a real war goin on between the fishermen 'n the fish: the oysters, the smelts, the clams, the quahaughs, the mussels. Only the whales, they haven' tried to catch. Heh!... with the kind of boat we got on our shores, catchin a whale!... It's like tryin to hoist a camel on a wheelbarrow.

But we ain't complainin, no sir... cause you still had clams, if you didn' get no smelts. Like I says to Gapi, it's always a year fer one thing 'r another. As if the fish didn' und'stand each other, 'n they came up the bay one kind at a time. Only one thing though, maybe they could figure out a way they was always som'n to catch down there in the water. Oysters, you see, are there in winter, but clams are jus' like bears, they come out in Spring. So us, when they ain't no ice... well, we eat pancakes 'n beans.

That's another thing I says to Gapi: What are you complainin about?... No smelts, well then, stamps, I says to him. The less smelts you have, the more stamps you get. This year, we been eatin off our stamps all winter. Cause the gov'ment can't let the poor folks go hungry, jus' can't let us croak on an empty stomach. Cause full-fledged citizens, we is, that's what the social worker tol'us, so all year long, we eat pancakes 'n beans... Nope... in Spring, by July almos', we got goose tongue, 'n some greens.

We set out on a small row-boat 'n go pick some on the sand bar.

I remember the first time, when we got married, we finished the weddin party by goin on the sand bar. I gathered greens all day 'n ended up with a twist in the back fer my troubles. Gapi, he was pickin goose tongue... A lotta years have gone under the bridges, but we still like that, better believe it!

Gotta admit, fer full-fledged citizens, we ain't short of not'n. I get up early in the mornin and I cook pancakes so we'll have some fer the day. Come night, they been reheated twice, so we eat'em with molasses to take away the funny taste. 'n Saturday 'n Sunday, beans it is. Everybody's got his blanket too. At night, after seven o'clock, I start shovin'em blankets in the oven fer a while, to heat'em up. Well, takes me all evenin cause by the time you got one warmin up, you got two coolin off, 'n you're ready to start over again. Goes on til they fall asleep, shakin all over like I was rockin'em. When the lot is asleep, I carry 'em to the same bed, young 'n older alike, 'n then, me 'n Gapi, we can go to bed. A real mattress with springs the priest gave us. If we didn' watch out, we could even feel'em springs goin through our backs.

In the month of August, we went to the picnic at *Sainte-Marie's*. Took our row-boat to go 'n we came back by truck. The truck à *François* à *Pierre* à *Jude*. Yep... a nice yellow truck fer carryin feed. So, we was sittin on shells to go, 'n on feed to come back. A real nice picnic, gotta giv'em that. They was all kinds of things on the ground: balloons, halos, *poutines*, game-stands, square dances, bingos, whistles, stew 'n donuts... they was not'n missin.

Ah! no question about it, it was what you could call a nice picnic. 'n on top of that, they was an agronomists' exhibition. Us, we'd never seen not'n like it, fer sure.

...Pr'cessions of calves, 'n pigs, 'n sheep, better believe it! Yep, seems you got farmers spendin all their time gettin their stock ready fer the exhibition. But once they arrived in *Sainte-Marie's*, the poor cattle was all frightened 'n edgy. Cause of the wheel of fortune 'n the merry-go-roun' spinnin over their heads. So, wasn' easy fer the judges to hav'em march in lines of two, like when we use' to go to school. Well, come to think of it, the steers 'n the colts looked a lot better than us. They'd fed'em, 'em ones, 'n fatten'em, 'n forc'em to grow fat all year so they'd look good fer the exhibition. Ah! fer that matter, nice hunks 'em animals was, 'n they sure looked like they got everythin they needed. Even saw a sow that was so fat, by God, I think the ol'gal must of been raised on cream 'n chocolate, I'm tellin you. Well, she's the one that carried off the big prize medal.

'n they gave a medal to the barber that was the fastest to shear a sheep; 'n to the rooster that cock-a-doodle-dooed the loudest; 'n to the turkey-hen that had the nicest tail; 'n to the woman that had the nicest blanket; 'n to the one that made the best molasses cakes; 'n to the cow that got the biggest dugs; 'n to the ox..., ah! yep, they also had a medal fer the bull; that's how they call an ox that's on duty 'n is the champion breeder. They had'm brought all the way fr'm the other side of Acadieville, that one, 'n they charged fifty cents a head to go 'n see him in his cage. Me, I didn' see him, but *Majorique à Nézime* got a chance fer not'n: cause he says to the agronomist, like this, he couldn' afford payin six bucks to see an ox, no way.

— *Fifty cents*, the agronomist tol'm.
— *Nope, six bucks*, Majorique says to him; *cause, you see, I got my eleven boys, beside myself.*

When the agronomist saw that, he tol' *Majorique* not to move. Then he went to get he beast 'n came back with it, so the ox could have a look at him...

That's what *Boy à Polyte* tol'us; but they ain't no guarantee it's a true story, though.

'n all of a sudden, right in the middle of the picnic, you'd see the president climbin on top of the table — no doubt he was a *Léger* from *Saint-Antoine* — then he'd make the people hush up, he'd keep silent 'n stop talkin. So we'd wait. 'n when we'd realize not'n was happenin, well we'd start shiftin our feet aroun' and mutterin. Then, the president would blow in his microphone 'n say: *one, two, three, hear me.* 'n he'd start yellin. But the wind was too strong 'n we didn' und'stand not'n. Didn' make no difference, though, cause they was always some lady parishioner aroun' the president 'splainin it all as he went along. That's how come we knew they was announcin supper was ready, chicken stew 'n *poutines râpées*, that is.

Yep, real *poutines râpées* fer supper, better believe it, 'n chicken stew, by the potful. Was all ladies of the parish that'd done that. It's on the previous Sunday that the priest climbin the pulpit would order the volunteers to come 'n boil their *poutines* in the church basement. The big deal is to know who's gonna have the biggest 'n the whitest ones; 'n who's gonna get the most chicken stock in his stew. Ah! a bunch of lady parishioners together in front of their pots, in the basement of the church, ain't easy. Cause to beat the one next to her, each one would add more stock, 'n more *râpure*. They'd end up havin so much *poutines* 'n chicken stew, they'd hafta throw some of it away. Cause on that day, they can't give any to the pigs, since they are in the pr'cession. Seems they taste real good 'em *poutines*, 'n also that stew; but they charge two bucks a head, 'n us... Well, still, we have our supper, not far fr'm the others, behind the school, sittin on the grass. Cause we bring our own food to make sure we ain't gonna be missin not'n that day. We even buy us some beer. 'n there's some that go fer a ride on the ferris wheel. Ah! nope, that day, they ain't not'n missin. 'n all our cheques are gone. The social-worker, she tol' us it wasn' a proper thing to do, but Gapi told her it was none of her business. So she didn' come back. Don't really matter, since we get our cheques anyhow. Cause of the elections.

Yep, they say in time of elections, we got not'n to fear fer our cheques 'n our stamps. That's cause durin that time, the gov'ment has more money than usual. Don't ask me where they get it fr'm. Gapi, he says... but you can't listen to Gapi, specially in time of elections. Some says the gov'ment is pretty well off. Do you think that's true? They say if we went nosin around their coffers... imagine that!... *la Sagouine* with her nose in the coffers of the gov'ment!... Heh!...

The nice thing about elections, is they don't come often... Only once every four years. Sometimes they come after two years, but then, you can say things ain't goin right, so they ain't too generous.

Cause when one side is sure to win 'n the other side sure to lose, ain't no need fer promises, one way 'r the other. 'n us, we're sure to lose. But when a person ain't too sure, like this time aroun', ah! then, hold on, yep... promises are gonna fly all over. You gotta know 'bout that, Gapi says, gotta get into the swing of politics, if you don't wanna be losers. So us, we stay on the swing. We stay right there where the gramophones, 'n the electric irons, 'n the beer bottles, 'n the other promises pass by. They give you all of that fer not'n, cause you is full-fledged citizens 'n you got a right to vote. They even come 'n get you in a truck. Sure thing, by the truck-full... fer that matter, they ain't short on spendin. We drive aroun' all day in'em trucks, 'n we drink beer. But we always end up on the side of the loser, cause that's where you get the biggest promises 'n the nicest gifts... Don't really make much of a difference: whether it's one side 'r the other, once the elections is over, the gov'ment don't have no time to bother with us anymore. Sometimes, they even come back lookin fer their electric irons 'n their gramophones. Take back yer promises, we tell'em, but if you wanna have yer beer back... heh!... they never was an election candidate that asked fer his beer again.

...A good year it was. Not a single sudden death aroun' here. The late *Joe Caissie* died of lung disease, but he'd been tooberculous fer years. 'n *la Célina*, she had that kind of cancer that don't cure. *Ludger* à *Nézime*, well he drowned, it ain't what you can call a sudden death. When he realized his wife wasn' comin back, that she'd pretty well left fer good with her brother-in-law, he got'mself drunk jus' like a man can get'mself drunk, 'n he walked to the end of the wharf 'n jumped. He'd told *P'tit Jean* all about it, the night before, but the other one didn' believe'm.

Water's too cold, he says to him. That's why he drank'mself stiff so he wouldn' feel the water. In the month of April, imagine that! You still have ice under the bridge, in April. Could of very well split his head on a block of ice, he could. But nope, in that he was lucky, he went under right between two blocks 'n he drowned. They found'm on a sand bar, bloated like a pumpkin. He'd been too depressed, poor *Ludger à Nézime*, too discouraged. Had to end up that way. In a hole beside the cemetery... Sure enough. The priest didn' wanna bury him in holy land, cause he'd drowned 'mself. Seems it's forbidden... Gapi, he says forbidden 'r not forbidden... once a man is dead. But you can't listen to Gapi. When a man is dead, won't hurt him none to be blessed between'em six candles, in front of the church, 'n to have his hole in holy land like all self-respectin people. That's what I tol' him, Gapi, 'n I would of liked to say it to the priest if it wasn' so hard talkin to a priest when you don't got no education. Cause *Ludger*, so the priest says, he hadn' paid his dues either, 'n it wasn' clear if he'd done his Easter duties. 'n to go 'n throw 'mself down the wharf on top of that... poor *Ludger à Nézime!* A person's gotta be pretty down in the dumps 'n discouraged... If he could of known they wasn' even gonna let'm have his share of holy water 'n holy land to complete his eternity... maybe he would of tried to hack it a little bit more 'n end up dyin a natural death, on his mattress. Maybe then the Good Lord would of felt pity fer him... maybe... a person can't know fer sure... They ain't nobody that ever came back to tell us. 'n even if one came back, he sure wouldn' appear to *la Sagouine*. Us, we ain't no *Bernadette Soupirous*...

...Jus' poor folks, we is... jus' people fr'm below. But that ain't reason fer us to complain. As long as

we got our smelts, our pancakes 'n our beans; kindlins in the cove to heat us below zero; 'n no newmonia, no sudden deaths, but picnics at *Sainte-
Marie's* 'n election promises... that's what I call a
good year, 'n fer the new one, damn it, I wish you
jus' the same, yep!

V

_____ THE LOTTERY

Jos à Polyte jus' won the lottery! Yep!... as sure as I'm here, Jo's the one that carried off the first prize. Ain't too often we get a chance like that, aroun' here. Let's grab it while it passes. The first big winner fr'm aroun' here since *Frank à Thiophie's* lottery.

...A few years ago, that was, but none of the folks we know forgot *Frank à Thiophie's* lottery. Each one remembers that p'ticular event like the day he was born, that's fer sure! A hundred thousan' bucks, would you believe it! You could say we ain't use' to bein hit over the head with bags full of dollars, no sir. 'n when they come at you like that, a hundred thousan' at a time, he came pretty close to losin his marbles, poor *Frank à Thiophie.* They hadda plunge his head in a bucket of vinegar. Sure remember it, I'm the one that got the vinegar to pr'serve my cucumbers.

...Poor Frank! I'd say he's the luckiest man in the world to be born in a fishin-shack. He couldn' suspect luck was waitin fer him. Besides, he hadn' even bought the ticket 'mself. It was Dominique's missus that gave it to him cause he'd been weedin her string-beans all afternoon. If she only could of known, Dominique's missus, that it was the lucky number, she would of taken her gloves off 'n done her own gardenin 'erself. But she couldn' know. So she says it wasn' fair, a hundred thousan' bucks fer three rows of string-beans. The law had to get into it. But fer once, it was the poor folks that won.

...Poor folks... a manner of speakin that is, cause *Frank à Thiophie* jus' ain't what you can call a poor man. Maybe that's why the law had some respect fer him. You should of seen it: it was all *Mossieux Colette* here, *Mossieux Colette* there... wasn' any damn bit of *Frank à Thiophie* left, but only Mossieux *François à Thé-o-phile Colette*. Was even hìm, *Mossieux Colette*, that paid it all, the judge 'n the lawyers, 'n he also paid his taxes to the gov'ment, right then 'n there, in front of everybody. With a hundred thousan' bucks, he sure could pay some, don't you worry, 'n with that kind of loot, it didn' even hurt, almost.

Frank à Thiophie, he could buy 'mself a lotta things 'fore it started showin, yep, a lotta things... In the beginnin, he was so flabbergasted, didn' know which way to go. But wasn' long he learned. They soon came a bunch of people to see'm 'n sell'm all sorts of stuff. First thing he bought, I remember, I was there, was a tractor. Considerin he'd jus' won the lottery weedin string-beans, the salesman 'splained to him a farmer like him hadda own his own tractor. 'n he also sold'm a combine, you know, one of them machines that does it all: it plows, plants, weeds, cuts 'n picks it up, it does... Ah! fer a man that didn' have a field of his own, you'd have to say this, he had'mself one hell of an outfit, *Frank à Thiophie*.

So then, he hadda buy'mself some land, 'n farm buildins to shelter his machinery. That took money, 'n one thing he had, Frank, it was money. He bought'mself a washin-machine, a fridge, a gramophone, the whole thing el'ectric. We went there the first night to see the machines runnin, 'n to listen to the gramophone, but they wasn' workin, none of them, cause *Frank à Thiophie*, he had no electricity at home.

Not too long after that, they came an insurance broker. Us, you see, we'd heard about it, but we'd never seen one. Insurance brokers jus' wouldn' come aroun' here. But then, they started comin like they was makin up fer all the time they hadn' been aroun'. Every night a new insurance broker would come over, pullin out of his briefcase loads of papers all written out in advance, where all you had to do was sign yer name 'r draw an "X", 'n you found yerself insured fer life. 'n each night, a better one would come; 'n so, after ten days, he was insured way over his head, *Frank à Thiophie*. His teeth, his fingers, his life, sicknesses, robbery, fire, 'n even his children was insured, an ol' bachelor like him. It was guaranteed nobody could touch'm without havin an insurance company givin'm a refund. But they was no need fer no refund cause a rich man, you don't touch'm.

Only the dentist touched him. He fixed him up with three rows of gold teeth in his mouth, after that, poor Frank could hardly move his jaws. So one day, he flung his dentures down the drain 'n stayed with a hole in the face that left'm all deformed, poor Frank. He also went to see a rubber 'n a bone-setter. Seems like they rubbed 'n set more bones than he really had in his body cause he came back crippled 'n hunch-backed.

But he soon got the hang of it, ol' Frank. Even 'fore Spring, he was already actin big. Yep! Stopped

chewin tobacco 'n started smokin cigars 'n they even
was some big mouths spreadin aroun'... but you jus'
can't believe in the tales of some of them gossips...
they says *Frank à Thiophie*, he'd roll his cigarettes
with dollar bills. Now, that don't make no sense,
spreadin aroun' stories like that! Like Gapi says,
lucky 'r not, nobody here is gonna start makin any
smoke with the Queen of England. Anyway, since
that lottery of his, ol' Frank didn' roll his cigarettes
no more, he bought'em ready-made at the store.

And he got'mself some new clothes. Ah! not at
Arvin's, no sir. Bought'em clothes in town, ol' Frank.
Couldn' dress'mself like the common lot, now, could
he! Cause they tol'm, it's the clothes that makes 'r
breaks the man. So Frank, he looked aroun' him 'n
took off his clothes. He grabbed his mackinaw, his
overalls, 'n his rubbers tied up with a rope, 'n he
went to town. That night, when he got off the bus
'n walked across the village, even *la Sainte* didn'
reco'nize'm. A yellow shirt, a necktie, a hard hat,
shoes that squeak 'n pants that was striped crosswise...
he looked pretty much like a guy fr'm the States.
Ah! well, jus' you put some nice clothes on a tramp,
'n you almos' won't be able to tell the difference,
no sir, the difference between him 'n a senator. Sure
thing! They even fixed him up with double vision
glasses... couldn' see a damn thing, but he sure
looked good. A real school teacher. Some folks even
started invitin'm as speaker. Ah! In'em days, *Frank
à Thiophie* was no chicken-shit no more. Like Gapi
says, sure's educatin a hundred thousan' bucks.
Seems it's the Richelieu that invited him at their
banquet 'n asked him to come up with a few words.
Cause the Richelieu is a group of rich folks that
takes care of the poor ones. 'n now that Frank
had become a rich man, they got to thinkin him also

would have som'n to say 'bout poor people. Ah! fer that matter, he sure would of had som'n to say, ol' Frank, don't you fret, but at that time, he still had'em gold teeth in his mouth 'n he didn' manage to say a single word. They gave'm a round of applause anyway since he was the guest of honor, even though he never had no honor in his life.

Frank, he'd never had not'n in his life. He wasn' use' to not'n. But, he could learn. Bit by bit, a person can learn just about anythin. So good ol' Frank figured he could pretty well learn how to drive. Yes sir, cause there, you see, they also was Jo's garage that was itchin to sell'm a few things, to *Frank à Thiophie*. They sure would of liked sellin'm gas 'n oil. But ol' Frank, he was on foot. So they started by sellin'm a car. Dominique's Buick, it seems, 'n it was jus' like new. They only changed the wheels, to Dominique's Buick, 'n also the top, the paint 'n the engine; so it was like new. Well, it didn' stay new fer very long; cause they forgot to tell Frank where the horn was. So that on the first night, after hangin his foxtail 'n his three dolls to his windshield, 'n loadin the back-seat with all of the town's young crowd, well, seems ol' Frank didn' set his wheels straight, 'r maybe his windows was dirty... in any case, poor *Frank à Thiophie* swore he never saw the nun's cow. Well, they was those askin 'emselves what the hell he was doin with his brand new Buick, smack in the middle of the convent's corn field. But you see, Frank jus' wasn' use' to things. 'n when he saw the barbed-wire fence standin in front of him, the thought of stoppin 'r turnin back didn' come to him. His legs was too much in the habit of jumpin fences, 'n they says poor Frank, he stepped on the gas. Well, seems the nuns only charged'm fer the cow, the fence, 'n fifty bushels of corn. As fer the garage, they took back the Buick almos' fer not'n. Cause they tol'm like this, that if they was to fix it, it would cost'm five hundred bucks, 'n it jus' wasn' worth it no more. So it was better fer 'em to take it back. Gapi, he always had som'n to say about that... but Gapi, he's always gotta gripe.

It's like the story of the Black 'n Chinese babies. When the missionary nuns came by fer that Save the Children crusade, they wanned to know where *Mossieux François Colette* was livin, 'n they went directly to *Frank à Thiophie's*, 'n they made'm und' stand how he could manage to save some souls. He only had to pay twenty-five cents. 'n they made'm und'stand he didn' have to be bothered with not'n, not even havin the Black baby 'r the Chinese one come over here. They'd take care of everythin, 'em missionary nuns: they'd buy, baptize, raise 'n save a pagan fer twenty-five cents, better believe it. 'n they told Frank like this, the more he paid to save souls, the better the chance to save his own. *Frank à Thiophie*, like everybody else, had a few guilty pangs cloggin his stomach at night, so he started buyin Chinese babies 'n Black ones too. Each time they'd remind him of another sin in his past life, he'd add another soul to his list. He ended up ownin several tribes, ol' Frank, 'n like Gapi use' to say, they could of made'm Prime Minister of China 'r Africa. But it didn' help his guilty conscience, the miserable sinner. Cause a person, no matter how good he is, can always find one more sin deep in his soul. 'n I got a sayin of my own, that we're better off not to go diggin aroun' there too much. 'n Gapi, on that matter, was of my own sayin. Cause his Black 'n Chinese babies, they almos' made'm lose his marbles, poor *Frank à Thiophie*.

'n that's when Frank started gettin some bills. All cause one day, he'd tol' *la Sainte*: *"Go get yer hair curled, 'n I'll pay fer it."* Well, she didn' waste no time, *la Sainte*. All over the head she had'erself curled. Well, when *Laurette à Johnny* saw that, she wasn' about to stay with that bun of hers. We all went through the same thing, 'n'em ones that was goin to the doctor, the dentist, the rubber 'n the bone-setter, 'n that couldn' pay, well the doctors would jus' send the bill to *Frank à Thiophie*. It came to a point where ol' Frank, he couldn' keep up with all of the envelopes he had to seal. They also was the Boy Scouts sellin apples, 'n the priest passin by fer the church dues. 'n would you believe that way up fr'm the pulpit, the priest actually said *Frank à Thiophie's* name! He wanned to thank'm publicly fer the church bells Frank had paid out of his own pocket. Yep! Twenty-two beautiful bells swingin along all together 'n playin Christmas tunes all year long. They call that chimes, 'n it's *Frank à Thiophie* that paid fer'em.

'n when the month of August came aroun', Frank leaned on his barrel 'n started wonderin. Was 'bout time he bought'mself the thing he liked the most, 'fore he was left with not'n. Cause up to now, he hadn' had time to think much about'mself. Well, the thing he'd always wanned, *Frank à Thiophie*, was a house, a big house of brick-sidin, with a top floor 'n a bottom floor, a cellar 'n an attic. He also wanned his out-house inside, 'n hot water 'n col'water, a pantry, a big room, 'n a summer kitchen apart fr'm a winter kitchen. That's what he wanned the most, a big house, with a veranda all aroun' where he could sit on his rockin chair all year long 'n watch people passin by.

So he had it built, that house of his. A lot of
contractors came over with their plans, 'n carpenters
too, 'n they built him the whole thing within two
months; the attic, the out-house, the pantry, the big
room, the cupboards, three chimneys, 'n the veranda
all aroun'. It was the nicest 'n biggest house anybody had ever seen. They came folks all the way
fr'm *Saint-Norbert* 'n *la Pirogue* to see it. Ah!
Nobody felt like spittin on *Frank à Thiophie*, no
more. He'd become a big man commandin respect.

Well, one day, a couple of months later, he re-
ceived fr'm the gov'ment a kind of big thick
envelope full of pink 'n green papers. Well written, it
was, English on one side 'n English on the other, so
that a person didn' need no glasses to read it. Written real good... but nobody aroun' here could figure
out what they was tryin to say. So, *Frank à Thiophie*
went to see the priest with his thick envelope, 'n
the priest took'm to his office 'n sat down. Frank,
he kept standin here, on this side of the desk, watchin. Finally, the priest 'splained it all to Frank: 'n
when Frank realized how much he had to pay, he
also realized he was gonna lose his house. A pity it
was, he hadn' lived in it fer more than three months.

...It's jus' that he had not'n left, ol' *Frank à
Thiophie*. Not a single buck. 'n since he kept gettin
bills fr'm all over the place, he hadda let go his
insurance policies, 'n sell his machines, 'n the tractor,
'n the gramophone. They ended up unpluggin his
telephone 'n cuttin off his electricity. He had not'n
left, 'n he went back to his fishin-shack. That's where
he died, last Spring. When we heard about it, we
all came out to hear the bells toll Christmas
tunes on the chimes. Well, they didn' toll fer him,

cause *Frank à Thiophie*, seems he hadn' paid his dues, lately...

Well, don't you wait fer me, now. I'm goin over to see *Jos à Polyte* that jus' won the lottery.

VI

THE PRIESTS

I'm gonna tell you som'n... Yep... *Sagouine* 'r no *Sagouine*, I'm gonna tell you som'n... Oh! I didn' travel much in my short life, nope, 'n it ain't that I saw a lotta things, either. It ain't that I'm an expert, nope... I can sign my name 'n make out what's in the Gazette when the news is in French... But I'm gonna tell you som'n anyway: you musn' talk against the priests: rep' sentatives of the Good Lord, they is. 'n it brings bad luck. You saw what happened to my cousin *Caï* 'n to ol' *Yophie*? They never was worse backbiters of priests than 'em two scoundrels. I'm tellin you. The devil 'mself didn' come out of there with his feather in his cap. 'n if anybody likes to chew up a priest real bad, it sure's him. Well, you can sure see what he looks like. Nope, it brings bad luck, I'm tellin you.

Take my late father, he's been dead close to forty years now, 'n he almos' reached his eighties. Well, my father 'mself use' to tell us when we was young, we shouldn' get mixed up in the affairs of priests... That's cause they'd been some stories runnin aroun' the parish about this priest that had 'mself two servant-girls. So what? my father had tol' us. Jus' cause a man has two women in his house, is that reason enough fer us to start sayin som'n against that? 'n about his rectory, ain't it big enough to house all the women of the parish, not to mention the men 'n the children?... Ah! fer that matter, they was enough room to house calves 'n pigs in that rectory. 'n all made of bricks, that's right, real brick bricks, none of that limitation paper. Ah! fer a rectory, that sure was a rectory, you couldn' say not'n against it.

They use' to say that each first Friday of the month, it sure would get crowded in there. The priests 'd be comin fr'm all over to confess the folks. You had the one fr'm *Chocpiche*, 'n the one fr'm *La Prairie*, fr'm the Cape, *la Pirogue*, 'n *Saint-Hilaire*... Ah! I'm tellin you, they was such a bunch, they soon had the whole parish all combed out. We'd get outta there as pure 'n white as sheets. It wasn' a big confessional. A box the size of three lobster cages. Now jus' you try 'n dig out the sins fr'm yer soul when you're trapped in a lobster cage... Heh!... We could squirm all we wanted in there, 'n try hard to see som'n through the screen... a kind of thick grill made of hardwood, with cellophane behind the bars so we wouldn' stink out the priest. Cause it seems some young priests couldn' stand the smell of feet 'n they'd have a faintin fit. Wasn' use' to our smell, the poor souls, they lived in their nice rectories, scrubbed clean all year long, where it would only smell of Bon Ami 'n Lemon Oil. A priest jus' wasn' use' to our dirt.

Ah! fer that matter, we wasn' gonna shove it right under their noses either. When it was too crowded, we didn' go to church. We tried to do our Easter duties so we could be buried in holy land. We'd also give som'n fer the church dues. With yer Easter duties 'n yer church dues, you was all settled fer yer hole in the graveyard. As fer the rest, you could always manage... well, almos'... Gotta say, sometimes it wasn' easy. Specially confession, cause of that firm resolution. Yep! when the priest wants to know if you firmly resolve not to offend Thee... it's

almos' like he was askin you to change yer whole
life. But how does he want us to change our lives?
We ain't rich 'n we ain't got no spare life.

...Ah! let me tell you, it ain't easy, ain't easy at
all. When they says to us: "Stop brewin home-made
beer in yer cellars", well, where do they want us to
brew it? 'n we don't got the dough to drink som'n
else either. We don't got the dough to buy us some
wine, 'n rum, 'n a drop of that stuff in a stemmed
glass with a cherry soakin in it. It's home-made beer
fr'm our own cellars 'r not'n at all. They also want us
to stop swearin and doin' sinful acts in front of the
kids. Ah! now about swearin, I tol' the priest right
then 'n there in the box: about swearin, you're right.
God Almighty, don't make no sense swearin like
that. Jesus Christ, we don't even know how to speak
English. As fer the other thing... it's pretty hard... it's
pretty hard not to do 'em sinful acts in front of the
kids when you only got two beds in the house 'n
both of them is almos' one on top of the other. We
kill all the lights 'n... ah! it's pretty hard.

Ain't easy to 'splain that to the priest. Us, we
ain't educated, 'n we don't talk fancy, so we don't
know how to put it. The priest, him, when he
preaches, he talks like the doctor's missus, shellin
out some big words he can turn into a mean sentence.
They call that literature. Us, we ain't never seen a
speck of literature in all our lives. We talk with the
words we have in our mouths 'n we don't go too
far to find'em. We got'em fr'm our fathers that got'em
fr'm their forefathers. Fr'm mouth to ear, you could
say. So, it ain't easy to talk to the priest.

Sure would of liked to 'splain to'm how come
my daughter didn' get married right away. How the

hell did you want her to get married, she didn' have
a pair of shoes to wear. 'n·as fer the white dress,
she hadda wait fer her turn. They was only one
weddin dress aroun' here, 'n *la Sainte's* daughter
had already put up her bans. My daughter was
forced to wait fer her turn. But by the time the dress
was available, my daughter wasn', cause she was
pregnant 'n it didn' fit her no more. So we hadda
wait fer the baby to be born. Heh!... The baby
turned out to be twins. 'n so, when the future
husband saw that, he ran away. Poor *Angélique* had
to find 'rself another one. Now jus' you try 'n come
up with a young man nowadays that's willin to go
through that sacrifice with a pair of twins on his
hands! 'n twins that ain't even his... Ah! ain't easy.
'n when you get outta the confessional havin confessed all yer sins 'n all the ones of yer man 'n all the
ones of yer children, well you sure can't say you're
anxious fer the next first Friday of the month to arrive.

        And as fer that poor priest, you also gotta und'
stand'm. Ain't easy fer'm to know what's that you're
tryin to tell'm. Him, he ain't been raised like you
have. Ah! it ain't that they was all rich folks in
his house; but they still ate their three meals a day.
'n they slept in their own beds. 'n they got'mselves
educated. So, of course the priest, he reckoned we
oughta act like decent folks. One Sunday, he even
tol'us fr'm the pulpit that to have a pure soul, you
hadda have a clean body. Ah! fer sure... you oughta.
But try to keep a family clean fer twelve months when
it is buried in a shack all winter; 'n it digs clams 'n
oysters fr'm the mud-bank all summer. Try to learn
after that how to behave proper. So then, yer soul...
it's like the rest, you don't count on it. You musn'
count on not'n.

You gotta count on yerself alone to find salvation, 'r to make a livin. 'n it ain't easy. Cause you're
not always sure about what is good 'n what ain't. 'n
there's nobody to tell you. You'd have to rely on
rules 'n regulations. But sometimes...

...You folks didn' know ol' *Desroches*. He use'
to live by *le Chemin des Amoureux*, but it's been a
long while since he died. Well, ol' *Desroches*, he
spent part of his life outside the Church, cause they
had'm excommunicated. Yep. Ah! a helluva thing
that was. I sure remember it. 'n my father also tol'
me a lot about it.

It was the thunder's fault, my father use' to say,
the thunder that burned down the church. Others 'd
say it was the spirit of the late *Dollard* comin out of
it's grave to set it on fire. Some even claimed it was
the priest 'mself... but you can't listen to what the
gossips 'n the big mouths have to say. Nope, my
father always said you hadda blame the thunder that
fell like a bolt of fire.

Anyway, the church burned down 'n the people
hadda think about rebuildin it right away. But this
time aroun', the town folks said it had to be moved
at the Corner cause that's where the shops 'n the
post office was. But those fr'm *le Fond de la Baie*
wanned to keep it by the sand-dune, it was closer to
their homes. Now, what do you think would of been
the best thing to do, rebuild the church where they
was the mos' people, 'r where you had the mos'
folks close at hand? Ain't easy to tell. 'n the men
got to fightin.

Ah! fer that matter, the men would often fight
in'em days, 'n if it had all stopped there, nobody
would of had not'n to be sorry about. But it didn'

stop jus' there. Cause ol' *Desroches*, he was the one
that had built the church, the same that burned
down, he had built it 'n decorated it with his pocket-
knife. So he felt like it was almos' his. Now you try
'n take away fr'm a man the church that he built
with a pocket-knife, 'n then burn it down, 'n move it
at the Corner, without lettin'm have som'n to say
about it... He shook his fist at the priest, ol' *Desroches*
did, 'n he got 'mself excommunicated. 'n all his life
after that, he stayed out of the Church.

...Of course, a person don't have no right to
shake his fist at a priest. 'n it's obvious the bishop
has the right to excommunicate a Christian 'n
deprive'm of his salvation. But *Desroches*, my father
use' to say, he wasn' a bad man, 'n it sure was a
shame he had to burn in hell eternally jus' fer
havin lost his temper one night by the sand-dune.
So it's kind of hard to know sometimes who's right.
'n a person may start wonderin fr'm time to time if
the Good Lord 'n the priests always see eye to eye.

One time, they came a priest fr'm the ol'
country. A mission, they use' to call it. Seems they'd
been comin each year, but us, we'd never go cause
if we wasn' dressed good enough to be seen by our
own people, it would of been a lot worse to be seen
by 'em strangers. But that year, they said it wasn'
a priest like the others; a saint, that one was, a real
saint, the kind you put up on an altar. Seems he
made miracles, so we decided to go 'n see. Well, the
minute we got in, we figured he had reco'nized
us, cause way up fr'm the pulpit he said: "Blessed
are the poor, the hungry, the ragged, 'n the ones
that went to prison." We didn' know we was as
blessed as that... but anyway, we'd come to see.

Ah! as fer bein a saintly man, no doubt about it, he sure was. When a man walks barefoot on the snow 'n never eats no meat without bein forced 'n only cause he made a promise, that's enough to set'm up on the altar while he's still alive, damn it! 'n that one sure knew how to talk. He could preach you a sermon fer three hours without you hearin a pin drop in the center aisle. He was so good at tellin you 'em stories about Noah 'n Jonas, you could of sworn you was inside the stomach of the whale, right in the middle of the flood, I'm tellin you! 'n fer long stretches, he could say it all in Latin like a man who would of been born in Nova Scotia. A real saint. 'n the well-off women would haggle with each other over who was gonna invite'm fer supper. Everybody wanned to be cured of som'n, everybody wanned his own miracle. Us, we didn' stand a chance cause we couldn' have'm fer supper. So, I took the chance 'n I tried to see'm through the screen of the confessional. That's when I realized it was even tougher than und'standin the priests fr'm aroun' here; cause this priest fr'm the mission, he only knew about sins fr'm *Québec*.

And yet, one day, one of them came. He wasn' exactly a priest, that one, he was what they call a White Father. That's cause his cossack was different, all white it was, 'n I dunno if it could stand fer a real cossack. 'n we never saw'm confessin people, 'r preachin, 'r collectin church dues. It wasn' what you can call a saint either; he didn' walk barefoot, 'n he could eat baloney just as good as he could eat sausages, if that's what you would give'm... Yep, cause him, he would eat at our place. Ah! no big thing, that man wasn' a fussy eater, 'r the kind that raises his little finger when he drinks his tea. He would eat with us, he would talk with us, he would

play cards with us. 'n if we got a letter fr'm the
gov'ment 'r a notice fr'm the police, he would fix it
up fer us. He never gave us his mother's ol' clothes,
'r the broken chairs that was layin about in his attic.
Nope, but he would help Gapi to shingle his roof,
'r put seaweed aroun' the house, 'n saw up some
wood fer the winter. He wasn' a saint: he didn' do
no miracles, at least we never saw'm, 'n he wouldn'
tell us no Bible stories; though he could sure tell us
some funny ones. Ah! whenever he came aroun' our
place, it was like havin over my own father, 'r
l'*Orignal*, 'r *Pierre à Calixte*. With him, we didn' feel
ashamed, cause he wouldn' even notice that the
beans had been warmed up twice, 'n that we didn'
have no double windows, 'n no oilcloth, 'r brick
chimney. You could say he was jus' like one of us,
Father *Léopold*, 'n we didn' need to hide our lice 'n
our bugs whenever we saw him raisin his cossack
to jump over our fence.

...Well, one mornin he went away, he left fer'em
warm countries... to convert pagans. Yep!... It's like
Gapi use' to say: if they could only mistake us fer
pagans, one of these days, maybe they would send a
Father *Léopold* to us too, 'n he would talk to us, 'n
tell us not to worry about the last rites, 'n send us
straight to heaven after our final death. But you see,
we can't all be pagans, so us, we're still waitin to
see if they wouldn' be aroun' som'one to open the
doors of eternity when we get there.

VII

THE MOON

Nope, they ain't gonna convince Gapi they sent a man to the moon, a man with two legs, two eyes, ten fingers 'n a nose, takin a walk on the moon, in this day 'n age. Nope, that's too tall a story fer Gapi! Ah! frogmen, yep, 'n apemen, sure, all you want, he says. But a man on the moon, not'n doin. On that matter, he's gonna stick to his point, Gapi. It's no use tellin'm the newspapers had his picture on the front page with his moon under his feet, all in livin colour, nope, it's too tall a story fer Gapi. It's all propagation, he said: they make all that jus' fer propagation. A man on the moon! he said, peuh! All right, all right, don't blow yer top, I tol'm. If you don't wan'em to go to the moon, they won't go, that's all... Ah! Gapi, he ain't easy.

A man is made to walk on earth, he said, 'n it's tough enough already walkin straight aroun' here, without us tryin to walk on stars. 'n why the hell would they go to the moon? Why the hell? Ain't not'n tò eat there. That's what they said. They ain't a cabbage 'r a turnip that can grow on that land. There's only sand 'n stone on the moon, they ain't an acre of good land, that's fer sure. So why the hell would they go through all the trouble of landin on land that ain't real, 'n that can't even give you a day's supply of food? If they didn' try to plough the dune cause it was only sand, 'n they gave it away to Arvin's fer a couple of bucks, do you think they'd go through all that trouble on the moon?...

It was no use tellin Gapi no one was arguin with'm 'n that he didn' have to shout. He was boilin mad. 'n he wasn' gonna let no one tell'm they'd sent a man on the moon.

Yep, Gapi couldn' take it either, when all the fishermen fr'm aroun' the bay sold their share of the sand-dune. All right, he said. You couldn' plough the sand-dune, it was no good fer potato fields 'r timber land. But it belonged to the fishermen fr'm aroun' here 'n they had no business sellin' it. Caus'if they sold it, Gapi said like this, it's cause they was a man willin to buy it. 'n how come he bought it? Gapi 's got a sayin that if a man wants to buy yer shirt, it's cause under yer shirt there's som'n worth som'n, 'n yer better off not sellin it. If that dune sand is good fer Arvin's, he said, it's good fer us. Well, Gapi talks that way cause he owned no share of the sand-dune. Cause he sure wasn' afraid of sellin' the plough his late father had left'm, no sir!

It's all propagation, Gapi said. That's all the gov'ments ever think about, their own propagation. 'n they try to screw us up. But they sure won't get Gapi to believe in their stories.

First of all, he said, the moon belongs to everybody. Jus' imagine now if everybody got it in his head to cut'mself a piece of the moon. If they was capable of cuttin down all of the trees fr'm the upper county to build their parks 'n their lumbermills, they sure as hell can cut up the moon so they won't be enough left by night to attract the smelts. 'n why should the moon belong to one man instead of another, anyway? It's like the air we breathe, they don't have the right to take it away fr'm us. But how do we know if one of these days they ain't

gonna start sellin us our moonlight? They sold us our
sea-water to fish in it, didn they?

...Ah! now there, Gapi 's right. They sell us our
fishin permits, 'n they don't let us fish all year roun'.
The sea belongs to'em, jus' like the land, 'n the
woods. We got not'n ours. Except fer the wind 'n the
snow: that's ours fer sure, 'n it's free. The wind, the
snow, the cold, 'n the water in the cellar. The sea
don't belong to you, except fer the one that fetches
you in yer own house when the tides is high. That
one sure belongs to you, 'n you'll have to get rid of
it any way you can. Only thing is, the sea that
rushes into yer cellar don't drag no lobster 'n no
salmon with it; jus' sea, foam 'n mud. Anythin that
don't pay is yers.

Gapi, he says like this, that if some men had
gone to the moon, well, the moon would now
belong to 'em, like a country in the ol' days would
belong to the one that found it first. I tol'm it ain't
like that at all. Usually a piece of land don't belong
to the one that finds 'n clears it first. It belongs to the
one that's strong enough to push aroun' the other 'r
rich enough to buy it. Cause if lands stayed with
those that cleared'em, wouldn' we still have our fifty
acres? That's what I tol' Gapi. Or else, wouldn' we
be allowed to fish all year roun' on the bay? 'n hunt
partridges 'n porcupines in the woods? Nope, that
ain't the way it is, nowadays. The land belongs to
those that can keep it.

Or to those that can keep it long enough. Cause
there comes a time when you gotta wait. If *Jude's* boy
had waited a shade longer, if he could of hacked it
a little bit more, he would of kept it, that bus of his,
'n today, he'd be enjoyin a good life; 'r at least, he'd

be supportin his family in his own country. But he
exiled 'mself too soon, *Jude's* boy. When he realized he was losin ground every day, 'n losin money
too, fear got to'm. It's jus' that he didn' have the
means of runnin into debt, *Jude's* boy, of doin a new
paint job on his bus, 'n puttin in some spring-
bottomed seats, 'n hirin 'mself a driver with a cap 'n
a police coat. 'n he also would of had to plan a
longer ride, up to Sussex 'n Saint John, so his
customers wouldn' have to switch buses in town. But
all of that took money, 'n you see, aroun' here... So
what happened is a man with lots of money came
over fr'm the States, 'n since he could afford it, he
bought 'mself a new bus with eight wheels, nice
velvet seats with an ash-tray in each one, 'n a shit-
house in the back seat. Ah! One hell of a bus, that
was, no doubt about it, nobody argued with that. 'n
the folks started takin that bus instead of the one
owned by *Jude's* boy, cause of the shit-house 'n the
velvet seats. Then one day, we heard *Jude's* boy had
sold his bus 'n left fer the States to work in'em
sweat shops. 'n now, well, we take the bus fr'm the
States to go to town. You see, if he could of
waited a little bit, *Jude's* boy, jus' a shade longer,
maybe he would of met with better times, 'n could of
been able to afford a shit-house in his bus... Ah! well,
ain't easy, ain't easy fer a man that's got not'n to
have som'n.

When the goin gets tough... anyone that owns a
piece of land should try 'n hold on to it 'n wait fer
the storm to pass. He should say to 'mself, it's only
a gust of wind, 'n it won't last. But nope, he's gotta
have som'n to eat right away, 'n support his family,
so he sells an acre, 'n another one, 'n then his
timber-land. 'n one mornin, he wakes up with a field
of weeds on his hands, 'n he ends up lettin it go to

the highest bidder. In'em cases, the highest price never means a good price. 'n a lotta times, it's the same one that buys the land of everybody. Where does that guy's money come fr'm, well... when a man's got money, he's got money, that's all. You don't go askin yerself where it comes fr'm. A rich man is a man that has money, that's all. So when the goin gets tough, like nowadays, everybody sells his last strip of good land, 'n picks up his papers fer the States, 'r starts goin on stamps. Then one day, you realize the whole upper county belongs to one man. 'n that one, he can do anythin he wants.

...If he wants, he can reforest all the good farms our forefathers have been clearin fer the past six generations. Yep, just about two hundred years of cuttin down trees 'n stubbin out fields, my late father 'mself told me so. 'n now, here they is plantin spruces on those lands. Soon, they won't be a village left in the country, but jus' wood like in the days of the Injuns. But the Injuns, they use' to live in the woods, it was home fer'em. They'd build their wigwams there, 'n they'd hunt fer beavers 'n part-ridges. Yep, they was at home in the woods. But us, it don't belong to us, none of it.

The whole country belongs to the one that paid fer it, strip by strip. 'n that guy, if he wants, he can forbid people to fish on the lakes 'n rivers; he can stop'em fr'm pickin blueberries 'n raspberries in the moors; 'r havin picnics in the woods; he can set up his "No Trespassin" signs all over the place. It comes out there ain't a single strip of land, 'r water, 'r post road where a person has a right to relieve 'mself without payin fer it... Well, that's what they would do with the moon, Gapi said.

Ah! well, as fer the moon, that's their problem. Don't seem to me we'll ever feel like relievin 'rselves up there. As fer the rest, we got not'n to say about it. It's much better that way, I said to Gapi. As long as they'll be busy up there, we'll be okay down here. Let'em fight over the moon, I tol'm. We should let'em fight anywhere they wanna, that way we'll be sure they'll leave us alone. If they wanna make war between 'emselves, I said to Gapi, in Egypt 'r in Vietnam...

But Gapi, he don't wanna believe either they is havin a real war in Vietnam. 'em stories, they is all made up, he said. Cause a war, it don't work out that way. Fer that matter, Gapi knows what he's talkin about, cause he went to one, in the ol' countries. 'n he says all they tell us about Vietnam, it can't be done. A war, it's fought between two armies, on a battle-field; not in streets 'n schools, with women 'n children. 'n what would the States be doin there in the first place, he said, in Vietnam? That place, it ain't their country, they jus' wouldn' of got mixed up there. They ain't a single American crazy enough to go fightin at the other end of the world, jus' like that, in a war that don't concern'm.

— Well, I said to'm, how come you went to England, then?
— Cause they circumscribed me, he said.

So then, I said to'm, maybe they circumscribed the Americans too. But it ain't with that kind of talk you're gonna change Gapi's mind. There's jus' no way he's gonna believe you got a war goin on down there. 'n if the Americans had gone all the way to a little ol' country like Vietnam, he said, a country so tiny it's as big as *la Barre de Cocâgne*, do you think, he said, that war of theirs wouldn' be over

yet? Ah! fer that matter, Gapi's right. Americans
ain't use' to havin their wars drag on, no sir. The
time they dropped their Titanic over Japan, not one
cat came outta there alive. Now, how is it they
would let a war drag on like that in a country no
bigger than *la Barre de Cocâgne* 'n even deeper
inland than *Saint-Norbert 'n Saint-Paul*? Gapi, he
says it's all propagation. Well, leave them alone, I
says to'm. When the soldiers will all be dead, 'n all
the bombs exploded, it'll be over 'n we'll be okay.
It's a lot better, I says to'm, that it's goin on in the
ol' countries.

Of course, the gov'ment mus' know it's better
to have it goin on in the ol' countries. That way,
ain't no danger fer us. 'n anyway, if they must at all
costs throw their bombs 'n train their soldiers to aim
good, there ain't gonna be no damage aroun' here.
It's the folks fr'm over there that are gonna get it all...
The women 'n children of Vietnam... Don't really
know what they done to us, 'em ones. Don't really
know... Ah! I reckon it ain't little people like us
that can know som'n about that. Sure won't be to us
the gov'ment is gonna start 'splainin why it declares
war 'n why it prohibits deep-sea fishin. Reckon it
ain't none of our business either. So, I figure the folks
that get killed over there, they mus' be people like
us, 'n they sure ain't the ones that have som'n to say
in this matter. They must of got stuck with a war, the
same way they took away our traps along the coast,
without warnin us, 'n without askin our permission.
Sure, I know the business of gov'ment ain't none of
our business, 'n we got not'n to say against it. The
folks fr'm Vietnam neither. 'n to start with, once
you're dead, you ain't got much to say, they know
that.

But Gapi, it so happens he's got som'n to say. Whether he's got som'n 'r not, he gripes. 'n he ain't plannin on lettin'mself get caught again fer another war, 'r fer the moon. If they need so'more folks fer the moon, ah! well then, they'll jus' have to manage without Gapi, he said to'em. 'n he'll stick to that, I know'm.

...Okay, okay: Gapi won't go to the moon, that's all. Nobody asked'm anyway. 'n I ain't got much hope either someone is gonna come 'n ask me to go on a little trip over there. But if they did ask me... oh! jus' a short ride to go 'n see... see what it looks like, a land so close to paradise, that ain't been messed up yet by no one, 'n hasn' been sold already to some rich folks; 'n with its woods still full of blueberries 'n its shores heavy with clams! Ah! it sure would be nice to see that! 'n watch the earth far away, right in the heart of heaven, spinnin aroun' night 'n day, with all of the people of the world on it. Fr'm far away, like that, seems to me a person can't really notice the mud in the creeks, 'r the poison ivy, 'r the couch-grass, 'r even the thunder 'r some mean twister. He can't hear the screamin kids, either... On the other hand, he couldn' hear'em laugh 'r call each other names. 'n he wouldn' see the wild geese flyin back in Spring, 'r the sap drippin fr'm the trees 'n rushin down river towards the bay.

...Ah! I reckon a person's better off stayin' home. Maybe he's right again, Gapi.

VIII

THE PEWS

Gapi, he don't talk often. More of a dreamer, he is. But when he opens his mouth to let 'em ideas behind his head come out, ah! then you better watch yer step: you can be sure there's a priest or a man fr'm the New Start that's gonna get som'n he ain't gonna like. That's cause Gapi gets his bile stirred easy. Bilious type they call that. Sometimes, turns yellow like a turnip, he does. Well, to each his own colour: me, they say I'm kind of green; Séraphine, with her pot of home-made beer, she's jus' about always red; as fer *la Sainte*, well the ol'hag has been blue since she started plannin to be a Child-o'-Mary. That's right, *la Sainte* herself now a Child-o'-Mary, can you believe that, the son of a bitch... Yep, pretty high thinkin some of them got. Ha!... If I would of let her, she would of turned into a nun, I'm tellin you!

Nope, Gapi, he don't speak often: but that's a time when he opened his mouth 'n let go a speech like no damn' bishop in the whole county could of come up with.

— *What in the name of Jesus Christ 'n the Virgin Mary, he says, can* la Sainte *have in her God forsaken mind!*

Now Gapi, he can be moody 'n pick a fight here 'n there, but he ain't an all-aroun' nut. 'n there's one thing he can't stand, 'n that's to see a man or a woman that ain't keepin her place. When Willy's

boy got 'mself a grade eight education, we ain't
had not'n against that, not'n at all. Not even Gapi.
Get yerself some education we tol'm, but don't you
come aroun' writin latin words on the walls of our
out-houses, you hear. *"Vincit"*, he'd written. Filthy!

So anyway, *la Sainte*, to this day, has her ribbon
'n her medal. You can bet yer life that, come Saturday
night, *la Sainte* is ironin her ribbon 'n rubbin her
medal with Saint Joseph's oil. Ah! sure changed her,
bein a Child-o'-Mary, changed her so much you can
hardly reco'nize her, I'm tellin you! fer a low-class
woman, that is. 'n that's what gets Gapi all worked
up. Child-o'-Mary, fine, he says, but that ain't reason
'nough to let her carry the big statue of the Goretti
durin the procession, 'n to figure you got a right to
claim yer pew in church.

In the ol' days, they maybe was a couple of
men havin a fight on the beach or behind the shop
of the blacksmith, but they sure as hell didn' clobber
each other right in the middle of the center aisle.
Now that, we ain't never seen. An' it's *la Sainte* that
started it all. What can you expect fr'm a Saint
anyway! An' we're the ones that is stuck with her.
One day, she got it in her head that she could go
to heaven like anybody else. 'n also that any ol'
place lik'a cellar or a closet jus' wouldn' be enough
fer her, wanned to be right there with all the other
Saints, she did, 'n the Angels, 'n the Lambs o' God.
Like, once on the other side, she wanned to be
sure she'd get a good seat, right in the front row,
to see it all; 'n that's why she decided to turn
religious 'n become a Child-o'-Mary. Nobody had
not'n to say 'bout that. But on the day she decided
to have her pew in church, well...

Fer as long as anybody could remember, they was some people that had their pews in front, 'n some others that had chairs in the back, 'n then some others that was jus' standin up. Everyone in his place. And they was no arguin. But sure'nough, on a good ol' Sunday in the month of August, the priest 'nounced fr'm the pulpit that on the following Sunday they was gonna be an auction in church. Seems that people fr'm the back-country had som'n to say 'bout what they called injustices. Wasn' fair, they complained, to always have the same folks sittin down in front of the others, 'n they got to thinkin the priest should auction off his pews. Well, let me tell you, it was easier said than done. Like almost all the parish was against it, except for those back-country folks 'n some outsiders. Us, well, we had not'n to say cause we didn't pay our dues. 'n when a person ain't payin his dues, well, he finds, like they say, that outside the church they ain't no salvation.

But on that day, we was all in church. Cause of the auction. Us, we never missed an auction, since it didn' cost not'n... except if you got yer heart set on buyin. But ever since the day young Polyte yelled: *One buck*! at Saint-Norbert's auction, jus' to sass'em, 'n then got stuck with a piss-pot, well, since that day, we go to auctions but we keep our mouths shut. Anyway, on that good ol' Sunday in the month of August, we went to have a look at the sale of the church pews.

They was all dressed nice 'n started with a procession fr'm the main tabernacle to the side tabernacle. 'n then, they explosed the Blessed Sacrament, and it stayed explosed fer the whole auction. Seems the priest wanned the Good Lord 'mself to keep an eye on the auction, so as not to let a pew go fer under five bucks. Well, the way Gapi says it, the Good Lord mus' be a sharp businessman cause He sure made a bundle that mornin. You should of seen it. Jus' fer the first two pews of the center aisle, they got more than thirty bucks. 'n why not: it's the wife of Dominique that started biddin against the doctor's missus. Five bucks once, ten bucks, twelve bucks, eighteen bucks twice, three times, sold! Sure makes a pew hard to get, at that price. 'n when the barber saw that, he wasn't about to stay behind *Basile à Tom*, that had jumped ahead two pews. 'n big *Carmélice,* she landed jus' in front of *p'tit Jean à François,* who decided right then 'n there to switch aisles 'n try fer the *Michauds'* pew. But the *Michauds* had been holdin on to their pew since Expulsion, and they had no intention to let go. Eight bucks, twelve bucks once... thirteen bucks, thirteen bucks once, twice, three times, sold, sold to *p'tit Jean à François à Boy à Thomas Picoté* against the *Michauds.* Ah! then things started lookin bad.

So we sat 'rselves in the choir loft, waitin fer som'n to happen. We knew the *Michauds* couldn' swallow that one. Sure 'nough. Would you believe they brought up the whole family 'n they landed in the pew belongin to the *Colettes* that was right in front of theirs. When the *Colettes* discovered that, it was too late: once, twice, three times, sold! So the *Colettes* swiped the one belongin to the *Maillets,* 'n the *Maillets* the one belongin to the *Légers,* 'n the *Légers* was just about to bid against the *Robichauds,* when we saw one of the boys of *Frank à Louis à Henri à Bill,* fr'm way back Saint-Hilaire, joinin the party in center aisle; 'n he was never able to attend mass fr'm a pew before.

Fourteen bucks! he yelled, right then 'n there, 'n loud 'nough to make the painted glass shake.

Ah! when the *Légers* 'n the *Robichauds* figured out what was goin on, they was so shocked they couldn' open their mouths fer a long while. 'n that's how come the back-country folks sneaked in the church 'n collected some of the pews. Cause when the *Village-des-Colette* saw the *Saint-Hilaire* stormin the pews, they came runnin too, bringin with'em the *Gallants*, the *Barthes* 'n the *Landrys*. 'n the Cove-folks jumped over the *Bourques*, 'n the *Petite-Rivière* bunch sent the *Cormiers*, the *Girouards* 'n half of the *Leblancs* flyin. The only ones left was the *Richards*, 'n they was sittin tight with their hands clamped on the back of the pew ahead of 'em, 'n you would of had to chop'em off before they let go. Well, they got the rug pulled fr'm under their feet, they did, 'n their breath cut short too, 'n by none other than *la Sainte* herself, would you believe it!

...Yep!... The good ol' *Sainte*, in the flesh, body 'n soul, bones 'n all, she stretched almost all the way to the altar, 'n there, without thinkin or askin not'n, she bought herself a pew. 'n it was the pew that belonged to the *Richards* since the foundation of the parish, better believe it! Right then 'n there, we figured all hell was gonna break loose. 'n sure 'nough, wasn' long. Everyone that got his pew swiped fr'm him that mornin had a grudge. 'n that was just about everybody. So when they saw the *Richards* ready to jump on *la Sainte*, they made the best of it 'n started clobberin their neighbours. In less time that I got to say it, the rungs of the chairs was flyin all over, the windows cracked 'n the Stations of the Cross was fallin on the heads of Saint Anthony 'n Mary Queen of Hearts. The priest was tryin to hold on the best he could to his censer, 'n tryin to pr'tect the Blessed Sacrament. As fer us, we was still in the choir loft clappin our hands 'n yellin: *Hit'm Joe!*

'n soon after, *Noume* fell on the organ that started playin *Sweet Adeline*. Ah! that's the best ceremony we'ever seen in church. 'n when, at last, the priest got everybody out, each one was holdin a piece of his pew.

Except fer *la Sainte*. She ain't got not'n, that one. Cause on the followin Sunday, when she put a feather hat on her head 'n went straight to her pew, it was already taken. 'Cause it ain't everythin, biddin at an auction, you also gotta pay, 'n pay cash too. See, *la Sainte* figured you could buy a pew on credit, like molasses. That's where she got caught. Cause the *Richards* had enough money on'em. And they got the pew. And that's how come a lot of the back-country folks had to go back to their chairs.

And that's also how come *Louis* à *Livaï* was left with not'n. Poor *Louis*! He'd been sittin in the same pew fer years, on the side of the Sacred Heart of Jesus, right by the pillar. Since the day he lost his wife, of lung disease that is, they was nobody left aroun'him, 'n he was bored, ol' Louis was. That's cause his children moved to the States, 'n left him by 'mself, yep, all by 'mself. So, when he was through with his chores, he went to church, *Louis* à *Livaï* did, fer a little while, every night. And in the mornin, he went to mass; 'n on Fridays 'n Sundays, he made the Stations of the Cross.

And he had his pew. A nice pew, with its step, its number, 'n a small shelf to support his mass-book. A real pew, like the others got. Ah! it ain't that he was a rich man, *Louis* à *Livaï*, or that he wanned to look important; it's just that goin to church gave'm som'n to do. 'n since he was spendin half of his time in there, he thought he might as well get 'mself a nice place of his own, where he could have a good view of the tabernacle, 'n where he wouldn' bother none. So, that year, he sold a calf 'n bought a pew. But the followin year, the pews had gone up, so poor Louis had to sell a cow. That's how come he lost most of his stock, *Louis à Livaï,* 'n he was down to sellin his poultry 'n his pigs. 'n then they was the auction. Now in that p'ticular year, a farmer came with his family to settle in the parish. They was supposed to be big farmers fr'm the South, these *Bourgeois.* 'n bein rich, they jus' couldn' be left standin up in the back of the church, durin the ceremonies, shameful that was. So, seems the missus told her man she wanned a pew right away, jus' like that. Well, kind of hard fer a newcomer to drive a neighbour out of his seat in church, the minute he joins the parish. Have to wait fer a pew sale, he says. Well, wasn't long they was an auction.

Meanwhile, the missus was askin aroun' to know who couldn' pay the full price fer his pew; 'n she got her man to bid against *Louis à Livaï.* Well, they didn' have to bid fer long cause ol' *Louis* had not'n left but a couple of chickens 'n a goat. 'n the goat, well, he had it since the wife passed away, 'n he didn' wanna get rid of it... So, he lost his pew, *Louis à Livaï* did, like a lot of the others. Seems he don't go back to church often, these days. Some say he stays fer hours, at night, sittin alone by his snake-fence, 'n doin not'n. Kind of makes you feel sorry fer him...

...As fer *la Sainte*, ain't nobody that was sorry fer her. Like she had no business tryin to sneak in with a crowd that wasn' her crowd, 'n tryin to live another life than hers.

— You gotta know how to keep yer place, Gapi told la Sainte. *The front pews are fer'em folks in fur coats 'n silk scarfs; 'n those that come to church wearin mackinaws 'n gumrubbers, well, they gotta be happy with the chairs in the back; 'n us, we gotta stand on our own two feet, like we always did.*

That's what Gapi told. 'n I'm tellin you, they ain't no bishop that ever spoke different.

IX

THE WAR

Lucky thing they was the war! What would we have done, all of us, without it? Ah! Times had become pretty rough. Between the depression 'n the war, they was an idle period where not'n was happenin no more. Not'n was happenin in 'em days, 'n we could of very well croaked like stray animals in their holes. But they was the war. Got here jus' in time, it did. Just in the nick of time to save us fr'm poverty. Cause if we hadn' managed to hold on till then 'n we'd died 'fore it got here, nobody would of noticed. Cause in 'em days, seems even the rich folks had a tough time makin ends meet. So us... well, us we couldn' even make one end meet. We couldn' make not'n at all. Lucky thing they was the war.

Yep... a real good war, I'm tellin you. Fore the war got here, I reckon the Good Lord 'mself would of had a lotta trouble if he'd been asked about the poor folks. He wouldn' of been able of namin us all, I figure. Nobody seemed to know they was still some people alive aroun' our place. Cause in the last years, the only thing that seemed to come outta there, was children's coffins. 'n those that couldn' die stayed buried like groundhogs in their hole waitin fer Spring to come. Well, our Spring was the war.

That's when we all got out. They would even come 'n fetch us in our homes. The war wasn' yet three months old, that they already knew the names of all the poor low-class men, with their age, their weight, the colour of their hair, the sicknesses they had 'n the ones they didn' have; they also knew what each of them could do, 'n how many wives 'n kids they had. It was all written down on paper as if fr'm now on, the gov'ment itself felt like takin care of our business... Kind of strange, that was, but we didn' complain. Cause it didn' make no difference who took care of our business, they couldn' take more than what we had, 'n we had not'n.

I remember the last thing we let go was our beds 'n our mattresses. Ah! no spring mattresses 'r feather beds they was, no sense in pr'tendin. A lotta times, we'd make'rselves beds with the planks you get fr'm schooners aground on our shores. They had that sea-foam 'n seaweed smell about 'em, but at least, they didn' take in water. 'n we made 'em high enough on their legs so we wouldn' jus' drift away durin high tides 'r when thawin started. Well, finally we had to let our beds go with the rest. Cause there's no way you're gonna eat box-mattresses 'n feathers. A person can sleep standin up 'r on the floor, but he can't eat no wood... not fer long, anyway... Not all his life... Lucky thing they was the war.

They came by jeep, one mornin, right up to our houses. Us, we didn' have no post road runnin by our front-doors, so they came by jeep. Real nice jeeps, all shiny 'n so strong they didn' have to bother with gettin off 'n openin the gate, they jus' rammed through the fences like they was a bunch of clothes-lines. All the men came out to see what was happenin and they found 'emselves faced with circumscription. They circumscribed them right then 'n there, on their own doorstep. 'n they went aroun' our shacks to make sure nobody was hidin. Well, I can't see why they'd be somebody hidin cause of some war goin on in the ol' countries no less than a hundred miles fr'm here. That's what Gapi told'em; but it didn' stop'em fr'm combin out our buildin's, includin our shit-houses 'n our fishin cabins. They didn' find no one, except fer ol' *Fardinand à Jude* that couldn' come out cause both his legs had been cut off higher than his knees durin the first war, 'n *Tit Coq*, that 'd lost a couple of marbles. He got struck with meningitis when he was young, poor *Tit Coq*, 'n like they say, they either die fr'm it, 'r they go crazy fr'm it. The poor soul, it left'm with a hole in the head. 'n so, bein the only one to be afraid of the circumscription, he hid 'mself in a barrel of molasses. They fished'm outta his barrel 'n they circumscribed'm with the others... Well, they hadda let'm go cause of what I heard, seems they found out he had six toes on his left foot.

They also let go *Julien à Pierre*, 'n *Tilmon*, 'n the hunchback. On one of them's report card, they wrote down he had his three lungs perforated: 'n another could only see with one eye 'n it seems that whenever they put a rifle in his hands, he would always be aimin at the sergeants; the hunchback, well they wrote down he couldn' fall into step; ain't easy to look straight ahead when yer eyes is bent on lookin down. Well, the poor folks that was saved fr'm joinin up, they came back feelin real bad, cause in'em days, the army gave good wages, 'n even sent cheques to the women that had their men at war.

That's when things started lookin up fer us. The first cheque to find its way here was the one fer *Laurette à Johnny*; 'n a lucky thing it was that the doctor was there that evenin, on account of the ol' gramma who was dyin; he was the one that saw it was a cheque, cause *Laurette* just about shoved it in the stove like any ol' ad fr'm a catalogue. 'n then, one by one, we all started gettin'em, 'n nobody else ever thought of throwin it in the fire.

Ah! fer a war, it sure was a good war! 'n a beautiful one. You should of seen it! When their parade would march through our road, all of us would rush 'n lean on the fence, 'n we'd stay there fer hours, watchin the tanks go by, 'n the jeeps, 'n the cannons; 'n we'd be yellin after the soldiers that was blowin on horns 'n beatin on drums. 'n we'd try to keep step besid'em. Good-lookin soldiers, neatly dressed as soldiers 'r sailors, with their heads shaved real nice 'n clean. They sure didn' make you sick. 'n they'd wink at you sideways, cause a soldier wasn' supposed to turn his head durin the parade. So we'd get in step 'n march besid'em. But they was always some crazy nut who'd risk pinchin one of them to make'm laugh, 'n we'd end up bein pushed away by the captain. Well, we could always listen to the music 'n watch the parade.

'n sometimes on Sundays, we could go see the Home Guard practicin war behind the church. Yep, cause in the Home Guard, they'd enlisted all the men that was too young, too old, 'r too disabled to join the army. It was what they called the army reserve, 'n it stayed home to defend us in case the war got too close. Those that was fit 'n strong, they'd send'em away to defend the others in the ol' countries.

Ah! a nice Home Guard it was, gotta giv'em that. It wasn' as nice as the parade marchin down the road, still, it was kind of a make-believe war they was doin in the church back-yard. There you could see *Tit Coq* with his six toes, 'n *Julien à Pierre*

with his perforated lungs, 'n *Tilmon* the hunchback,
'n all the ol' boys that use' to hang out at the blacksmith's 'n smoke by the anvil all day long. Now,
they was all enlisted in the Home Guard. 'n they
hadda sergeant to guid'em 'n show'em how to
defend the country in case the Germans dropped on
us by surprise. It was *Télex*: he'd already gone to
war, the first one that is, but he couldn' go back to
the battle-front cause seems he'd been gassed over
there. Left'm kind of close-mouthed, ol' *Télex*, 'n
pretty near the edge.

What the girls fr'm aroun' here liked best about
the war, well, I reckon it was the Flat Foots: that's
how we use' to call the English that'd crossed to this
side so they could come over here to practice fer
war 'n be safe at the same time. Cause they said it
was kind of hard fer a young soldier to be practicin
his war games while bein disturbed all the time by
bombs 'n cannons that... Ah! now there, Gapi found
som'n to say. You should practice fer war right on
the battle-front, he said, not behind the church. 'n a
soldier that tries to be on the safe side, he said like
this, I sure wouldn' count on'm. Well, fer that matter,
Gapi knows what he's talkin about. Specially since
them Flat Foots, well...

...They looked good, you see, real sharp. So all
the girls fr'm aroun' here wanned to have their
Englishman. Even the high-society girls. They made
no bones about it. But the Flat Foots was only here
to practice, 'n they went back home. A lotta girls
was left with their feelin's hurt... 'n one 'r two
more kids to feed. Ah! well, it still lasted fer some
months, 'r some years; 'n like I says, a person
shouldn' gripe 'bout happiness, even if it only lasts
a while. Jus' like the war, it only lasted a few years;

well, a real good thing it was, a real good thing! The best thing to happen since the depression 'n the shipwreck on the dune.

Well, yep, durin the depression, times got to be so bad, a person couldn' go any lower. But when you're low enough, like this, that's when they decide to do som'n so you won't croak. Fer instance, durin the depression, they invented the relief. Fr'm then on, we was all set. Each month, we got our bag of flour, our pot of molasses, 'n sometimes even buckwheat fer our pancakes. Depression saved us fr'm downright poverty. The worst time fer poor folks is when not'n happens: no war, no floods, no ecumenic crash... not'n to remind the world some folks don't got not'n to eat. The toughest times, they is. Lucky thing it don't last too long. Usually, there's a crisis of some sort every ten 'r twenty years, 'n so we can breathe easier every ten 'r twenty years.

The last time, it was the shipwreck. That mornin, more than sixty men was out on the high seas fishin cod. Seems the radio had forecast stormy weather, but our men they didn' have no radio on board, some of them didn' even have an engine 'n they'd be usin their oars. 'n so when they saw the storm already on top of them, it was too late to turn back 'n reach fer safety. Seems the waves was sixty feet high 'n you had some men on row-boats in there. Most of them ran agroun' on the sand bar, with their masts, their boats, 'n their backs broken in half. Fifty-three of them perished all at once. That was one time the priests didn' beat about the bush to bury'em in holy land. Easter duties 'r no Easter duties, if you perish in a wreck that claims fifty-three lives all at once, the're gonna bury you with the others in the graveyard reserved fer disaster victims. Ah! it sure ain't a happy day when you hear the bells toll fifty-three times the same day. Well, that wreck, it put us back on our feet fer a while. Cause the gazette, the radio 'n the Sunday sermon, they all started talkin about us 'n organizin collections to help us forget. Well, it did help us forget our hunger, fer a while, anyway.

Then they was the war. Fer us, I reckon it was the best thing. The best thing with the shipwreck 'n the depression. Cause they never stopped sendin us our cheques the whole time our men was on the other side. 'n the wives of the men that didn' come back, they kept gettin their widows' cheques. 'n *Caillou*, that lost one of his legs in England, he got more fer that lost leg than fer all the work he could of done with the other one. 'n *Jos Chevreu* that came back with two holes where his eyes was... well they paid fer his dark glasses, his white cane 'n they gave'm a pension. 'n then they was the kid of the dead *Pit Motté*: he wasn' even eighteen when they had'm sign up, 'n since the late death of *Pit*, he'd become his mother's bread-winner; well they found'm deep in the French countryside, two years after the end of the war, not knowin where he was, cause he'd lost his memory, the poor blessed child, when a rifle bullet stayed lodged right between his neck 'n his spinal cord. They brought'm back to his mother, the poor soldier; well, seems he hasn' reco'nized her yet.

Well, he came back at least! *La Sainte* can't say as much about her son: he got'mself married over there, 'n she never saw'm again, even though she knows he's still alive. They says he'll never come back. I reckon it's cause of Jeffrey's daughter. He sure had loved her, Jeffrey's daughter, 'n seems like

she didn' forget'm. They was promised to each other.
I reckon he can't make up his mind about bringin
back home a wife that could just as easily as not
take a walk under Jeffrey's windows jus' to bug his
daughter. Nope, It's absolutely certain *la Sainte* 'll
never catch a glimpse of her son again.

And maybe it's all fer the better. Considerin
what happened to poor *Joseph à Magloire à Louis*...
they had'm down as bein dead. So his widow didn'
waste no time: she gave up her widow's pension
'n went to live with *Damien's* second son, a good-
lookin lad in'em days, 'n he sure was a tough son of
a bitch. When poor Joseph came back fr'm the
war like he was a ghost, 'n he saw *Damien's* son in
his own bed... poor Joseph! Next Spring, they fished
him outta the sea with the oysters.

...That was twenty years ago. We're up to our
necks in poverty again. A war, it brings jobs, 'n som'n
to fill yer stomach. But it lasts five 'r six years 'n then
they make peace. After, we gotta go back to our
oysters, our clams, 'n our quahaugs. 'n times get
tough again. 'n poverty strikes. 'n there's only one
thing we can do: wait fer the next war that'll get us
outta this hole once again.

X

THE FUNERAL

We buried'm, poor Jos, buried'm in his miserable hole. Well, come to think of it, it didn' get done all by itself. Wasn' easy at all, but we buried'm, that's fer sure. That's over 'n done with. Poor Jos! We'd sworn so hard to him, you see. Ah! fer that matter, we'd sworn on all the Sacraments. Guaranteed him a hole, we did, a hole that was big enough to hold a coffin where he could stretch'mself out at full length, poor Jos, without havin to bend his knees 'r sprain his ankles. A real coffin with a pillow, a cross 'n handles, a nice coffin unholstered like fer a stiff with self-respect: that's what he wanned, poor Jos, that's what he wanned most in this world. We swore to him on the Virgin's head 'n on the ones of all the Saints we'd get'm a coffin where he wouldn' be ashamed of bein dead 'n restin beside the others, poor ol' Jos!

That's cause he still remembered his late father, Jos, 'n the first time he died. I'm tellin you. Around here, they always been sayin Jos' father, the late *Antoine à Calixte*, had died twice. How dead he was when he died fer the first time, well... Gotta admit he sure looked like it, anyway. It was 'bout the time of the Spanish flu epidemic, 'n *Antoine* 'd caught it like everybody else... 'n 'fore he knew what hit'm, there he was, stiff 'n ready to be buried. 'n since in'em days you hadda make it quick, so the sickness wouldn' spread aroun', they didn' waste no time in shroudin'm real good, 'n windin'm up in a clean sheet. That's how come *Antoine* wasn' a pretty sight 'n he didn' smell too good either. They was all sayin: we gotta bury'm right now, he's stinkin already. But that wasn' reason enough, cause *Antoine à Calixte*, he'd been stinkin all his life, the poor man. Well, anyhow, they took'm away, 'n jus' when they was singin to him his libératché; half his body popped out of the coffin 'n he yelled: "Jesus Christ! what the hell is goin on aroun' here?" At first, everyone thought it was the verger comin over to lock up the church — since cause of the epidemic, the funerals was after sunset — so all the heads did a sharp turn about. 'n that's when they saw the late *Antoine* sittin up in his coffin 'n tryin to free his fingers fr'm his rosary. Seems that when he woke up 'n realized what they was tryin to do to him, ol' *Antoine à Calixte*, he was cured on the spot. So much so that he never caught another sickness after that one, 'n it took a thunderbolt to knock'm out at age ninety-two, a thunderbolt that fell like a rock.

By the time his father died fer the first time, poor Jos was still young, 'n he never quite got over it. Cause on'em winter nights, he use' to hide behind the stove 'n listen to his father tellin about what he had time to see in the next world. All the folks fr'm up the hill would get together at *Antoine's* place to hear'm tell his story. You didn' have to drag it out of him, ol' *Antoine*. He'd tell'em all they wanned to know. You only hadda ask'm 'bout some person you knew 'r was related to, 'n sure enough, *Antoine* had seen him there, shovelin coal 'r followin a pr'cession of angels 'n sheep. He use' to say he'd seen in the hereafter the late *Pierre Crochu*, harnessed to the same cart as ol' *Bidoche*, 'n they was both pullin a load of devils, the same ones that come 'n tease the folks aroun' here on All Saints day. He also use' to

say the devil's boilin pot was full of folks fr'm home
that we thought was respectable 'n that would carry
their heads high in this world. But he'd say he
couldn' name them cause their descendants was still
alive, yep, 'n they still kept their heads high. The
late *Antoine à Calixte* was a great talker, he knew
how to scare the shit outta you 'r make you split
with laughter. But poor Jos, he wasn' laughin. Death
would give'm the creeps.

Seems it was aroun' that time Jos started thinkin
about it night 'n day. 'n the more time passed, the
more he tried hard not to let it sneak in 'n jump on
his back by surprise. He remembered his father's
first passin away 'n so, what he wanned, was a
respectable death, no unfinished business, no half-a-
death where you pop out of yer coffin with flowers
on yer head 'n yer fingers all tied up in yer rosary.
Nope. What Jos wanned was a death like the well-to-
do folks have. Them ones don't get buried 'fore bein
sure of drawin their last breath.

Problem was poor Jos had no money, he didn'
have a thing to his name. That's what troubled him.
To pass away real nice nowadays, ain't easy. They
gotta embalm you, 'n shroud you, 'n buy you a plot,
'n buy you a coffin, 'n find you some new clothes
to suit the coffin. All of that, you don't jus' find it in
any ol' place; 'n they ain't nobody yet that won a
coffin 'r a grave in a bingo. But poor Jos, he was
crazy about a beautiful death. Willin to do anythin,
he was. Well, he found a way. Yes sir, he took real
tough decisions, Jos did.

One day, he went knockin at the undertaker's
door. Once there, he asked to know how much it
would cost him to have a first class burial. Ah! he

saw pretty big, poor Jos! First class 'r not'n at all, he
says... Came real close to bein not'n at all. Anyway,
the undertaker took a good look at him, to see if he
wasn' joshin'm, 'n then started countin: the coffin,
upholstered inside 'n covered outside, six handles
'n a silver cross, big 'n small candles, the wreaths,
the curtains, the ribbon on the door, the blow-up
picture of the stiff... A hell of a thing, that was, cause
poor Jos, he'd never had his picture taken. 'n he had
not'n to wear to pose fer it, cause he still hadn'
bought his passin away clothes. So one of his cousins
lent'm a black coat 'n a white shirt 'n with them,
poor Jos went to see the phonographer. Three times
they took his picture. You see, Jos didn' want nobody
sayin he'd had his picture taken with his overalls on.
So he put the white shirt 'n the coat right over his
long-johns, 'n he tol'm not to shoot him any lower.
But, wasn' easy, cause seems each picture would
show below the coat a little bit of the long-johns.
Well they cut the picture right here, 'n poor Jos
looked like a real stiff. Sure did, they cut'm in half.

...Yep... a real stiff. But the thing that worried
Jos was that he'd already spent a thousan' bucks, 'n
he wasn' even buried yet. 'n then, they was his
grave. Cause with a fancy death like that, he hadda
have his own tombstone over the hole in the graveyard, ol' Jos. A real tombstone made of stone, with
his name engraved on it, 'n his RIP, 'n the date of
his death. 'n they even asked Jos what kind of death
he was countin on meetin, cause that too they usually
have it all spelled out on the tombstone. 'n they also
perch on top of the stone a kind of doll in the shape
of an angel that looks over yer last sleep. Now, all
that is pretty nice, but you gotta pay fer it. Cause
aroun' here, I never saw a man gettin his last sleep
fer not'n. Ah! dyin nice sure's expensive.

And then, you also have what they call a funeral. That's the burial ceremony: it's kind of a parade that starts at yer place with yer neighbours, the family, the priest, the choir-boys, the bearers 'n the stiff. They all walk two in line, behind the coffin, holdin their noses 'n snivelin... 'n there's no way that, durin a funeral, a person can start chewin tobacco, 'r laugh, 'r look back to see who's behind him. You gotta hold yerself straight, with yer head bent a shade sideways, 'n walk real slow. 'n you keep yer eyes ahead of you. 'n fer the funeral, you wear black clothes, 'n an arm band, 'n you take out a clean handkerchief, 'n you follow the parade, slowly up to the church, 'n the graveyard, yer eyes lowered. Then the priest buries the stiff in Latin, sprayin'm with holy water. As fer you, well you keep real quiet outta respect fer the relatives. Cause anyway you look at it, 'fore bein dead, a stiff was a man, 'n there's always someone left behind to mourn'm, 'n it don't make no difference what kind of scoundrel he was in his life. Ain't too common seein a stiff that don't leave behind a mother, a brother, a kid 'r a wife, that'll remember the days he was still young 'n strong, 'n followin' funerals with others. 'n that kind of memory makes yer stomach churn, it does, 'n brings water to yer eyes...

...But that don't last, cause the minute there's no more Latin, the grave-digger comes over with his shovel 'n the priest indicates to the people it's time to leave. 'n each one starts smokin again, 'n whistlin, 'n runnin, 'n yellin at his neighbour. The funeral's over 'n you can start livin once more.

...Well, you can live fer as long a time as you got. Cause you know fer sure that one day it'll be yer turn. Only thing is, you know you won't get a nice ceremony like that one, they'll bury you, sure, but without burial 'r funeral. ...Yep, ol' Jos was thinkin 'bout all that, 'n he had not'n, that poor man. So he went back to town with his picture, sat down 'n started reckonin. He reckoned all night. 'n the followin day, he went oyster-catchin as usual. But by nightfall, he hadn' come home like the others. Ol' Jos started workin double-time. Night 'n day, he'd fish. Everybody would tell'm: "Jos, you're gonna catch yer death." But, instead of slowin him down, that would spur'm on. The more he'd see death gettin closer, the more he'd fish, poor Jos. The others figured he was gonna clean up the bay all by 'mself. 'n they started goin after him. Poor Jos had to go more 'n more into the cove 'n up-river. 'n there, the oysters get to be few 'n far between, 'n he hadda work twice as hard... Well, poor Jos, they found'm one mornin with his head hangin over his boat, 'n his hands caught up in his rake.

...That's when the fishermen started feelin sorry fer all they'd done 'n said to him, good ol' Jos. It's as if all of them had killed him. 'n so, each one remembered the promise he had made to him, not to let the worms 'n the rats get ol' Jos 'fore the end of the ceremony. One night, on All Saints' day, we had sworn to him on Saint Joseph's Holy Oils that we'd bury him in a brand-new-never-before-used coffin that had handles 'n was upholstered 'n waterproof. Well, the only thing left to do was to keep our word. But it wasn' easy.

...Wasn' easy cause the late Jos, he had brothers 'n sisters. 'n when each of them got wind of Jos' death 'n of all he had started puttin aside fer his funeral, well they began arrivin fr'm all over the States, Ontario, 'n even the north coast of *Caraquet*

'n *Tracadie*, yep, some of them had reached that far!
Ah! they never was a man with more relatives:
brothers, sisters, cousins, godsons, a truckful of them,
they was. Well, they sure didn' get to church. They
ransacked his shack, his cellar, his boat, 'n they
took everythin away. Yep! They swept it all off, even
his black coat 'n his white shirt. To be buried, he
was left with his long-johns 'n his overalls, poor
Jos.

        That's when *Elie* had an idea. They sure as hell
hadn' taken away his shack, 'n his boat. It all
belonged to Jos, 'n it could very well follow him to
his final hour. It was a shack made of softwood,
the main thing bein it wasn' eaten away by worms.
So the men got to work on the shack 'n threw it
down. Then, they picked the best boards 'n they
repaired the outside of the boat jus' like new, so it
looked like a real coffin comin out straight fr'm
Arvin's back-store. 'n the women came over with
strips of curtains an they upholstered the boat all
in red'n white polka dots so it almost didn' smell of
fish at all in there. With the kitchen table, we made
a lid fer it 'n we hooked on each side the stove's
handles. Only one thing, we wasn' too sure that ol'
boat wouldn' leak, cause we all knew poor Jos use
to spend half his nights bailin out the water. They
was only one way to fix that, 'n that was to cover
the outside with brick-sidin. It was *Jonas* that agreed
to tear down the brick-sidin fr'm the south side of his
own house. His missus screamed all night, but *Jonas*
never budged. 'n so, poor Jos got'mself a nice coffin,
upholstered with curtains 'n covered in brick, with
stove handles all around, 'n his death picture
dressed in a black coat at the foot of the coffin. It
was the nicest kind of coffin the local folks had
ever seen.

But that ain't all: hadda dress'm up, poor Jos. He specially didn' wanna be buried in his overalls. Can you picture that, overalls in a nice brick coffin? Well, each one gave som'n away; 'n when we got it all together, we managed to dress'm up, ol' Jos. Ah! fer that matter, we was pretty sure he wasn' gonna suffer fr'm the cold in the next life. You never saw a man with more clothes on'm: three pairs of socks, four pairs of mittens, five shirts, two coats, four neckties, two pairs of pants, a cap, 'n three gumrubbers. 'n all of that, at the bottom of the curtains, inside the boat.

Yep... we took'm to church in a pr'cession, 'n we paid to have the bells toll. They even tolled half the mornin cause we'd given more money than we had to. 'n we dug'm a hole in holy land at the foot of the cross, jus' beside the nun's plot, a deep enough hole so the rats wouldn' get to him down there. As fer the worms, well Elie told us he'd filled the coffin with poison so they wouldn' dare come close.

...So, poor Jos, he's well pr'tected: he won't freeze, they won't eat'm, he won't pop out of his coffin either, cause we kept vigil over him fer five nights to be sure he was dead all right, 'n had no intention of comin back to life like his father did. Nope, poor Jos, he had no intention of comin back! When you get a funeral like he did, you take advantage of it, 'n you stay dead. Cause it ain't everybody around here that can get a first class funeral, with an upholstered coffin where you can stretch out all you want, 'n know that nobody's gonna come over 'n bother you fer all eternity. Damn Jos!

XI

THE GOOD LORD
IS GOOD

Sure, the Good Lord is infinitively good 'n infinitively kind 'n all sins offend him... 'n it's absolutely certain we're miserable sinners 'n heartily sorry fer havin offended thee... But, with all of that, can we die in peace? Is that enough to ensure the eternal eternity of a man? They says with yer scapular, yer medal 'n yer extreme unction, you ain't got not'n to worry about, 'n you'll have it, yer place in paradise. Ah! they ain't no guarantee you're gonna be sittin on Saint Joseph's lap 'r at the feet of the Child-Jesus-of-Prague. Maybe you won't have the best seat, but you'll have one, 'n that's all that counts. Cause, you see, if it's true, once in heaven, you can have all you want. Well, first seat 'r last... seems to me it don't make no difference.

It's jus' like hell. If you're about to go there, well I figure a little more live charcoal in yer bones 'r a little less... If you're burnin: seems to me you can't burn more than that. That's why once you're all set to go... well, I don't see why you should be holdin back. 'n specially since it lasts fer ever. You see, an eternity that lasts all the time, 'n that don't stop, it can't be lastin more 'r less: it lasts. So there too, I don't see no big difference between the first 'n the last place. To be burnin on a fierce fire 'r on a slow one...

...Ah! course I know the Good Lord is infinitively good 'n infinitively kind 'n that he's just. Has to be, 'r he wouldn' be a Good Lord. 'n I also know fer sure I shouldn' worry 'r even be wonderin... Cause they already tol'us that wonderin too much about religious matters makes you lose yer faith, it does. 'n once lost, seems not even Saint Anthony can help you get it back. So you gotta hang on to it with both hands 'n not let go. Hold yer breath, I says to Gapi, 'n don't let go. Soon as you're dead, then you can start breathin easy again: to believe, you won't need to see it all, you'll und'stand on yer own. Well, as long as we're still alive, we gotta believe in all what the catechism 'n the priests teach us, blindly that is, 'n with yer faith all tucked in the palm of yer hand, like it was the key to paradise.

We'll have to wait to be on the other side to und'stand. But boy, once there, we sure gonna und' stand! Ah! yep, we'll ask'em there to tell us every-thin: what's okay, what's a no-no; where it's okay 'n not okay; 'n how come the same things ain't no-nos to everybody; 'n what makes the priest decide to forbid one thing instead of the other; 'n why is it the priests don't see eye to eye with each other on the things that is sinful 'n the ones that ain't.

Like fer instance in my time, dancin was for-bidden in the parish, but not in the parish next to ours cause there, they was all Irish 'n they didn' have the same bishop we did. So the Irish 'n the Injuns, they could dance, 'n us, we couldn'. But one day, Jude's boy took out his truck 'n he announc-ed that if some folks wanned to give'm fifty cents, he would drop'em right at the door of the dancin-hall of Big Cove 'n then bring'em back the same night. We all jumped in 'n we had us a set of square dance that went on all night. They was *le Petit*

Maxime with his fiddle, 'n *Gérard à Jos* with his kazoo, 'n *Pierre Fou* tappin his foot on the floor. By the end of the evenin they wasn' a single Irishman 'r Injun left in the square dance, we'd taken over the whole floor. Ah! a helluva dance it had been! 'n all of that without committin even a single venial sin, better believe it. Whereas each time I'd dance with Gapi at home, I couldn' go to communion the next mornin. So the folks around our place thought the Irish 'n the Injuns, they was sure lucky to speak English 'n not to have the same bishop we had. 'n yet, he was a real good bishop, we had not'n to say against him... Well, he was a saint, 'n he didn' like dancin.

They was a lotta things he didn' like, our bishop. He didn' like beer, that's fer sure, cause they was too many folks gettin drunk in the parishes all aroun', 'n cause it didn' sit well with his stomach. They use' to say he'd throw up every mornin after mass, cause the wine would make'm sick. Well, a saint he was, 'n it didn' stop'm fr'm sayin mass all the same, each mornin the Good Lord brought. Lucky fer us, the Good Lord didn' have such a weak stomach though, cause He wouldn' of thought of inventin communion!...

They also use' to say that after his conformation rounds, the bishop had to take a bit of soda after meals, cause the poultry was too fat. Well of course, you can und' stand it ain't every day a woman welcomes a bishop; 'n a servant can be workin in a presbytery a long time, 'n be use' to seein fancy things, but when she feeds a bishop, well, she does her best 'n kills her fattest hen. Seems that in one single conformation round, he could gain up to twenty pounds, our bishop. But that didn'

stop'm fr'm conformin all the kids in the county,
yep! Cause he was a saint, he was. 'n he didn'
like women, our bishop. Nope, no backbiter could
never accuse'm of loose-livin, that one. Way up fr'm
the pulpit, he told us a lotta times that women was
an occasion fer sin 'n with'em you hafta watch out.
Every priest says the same thing. They even was one
that distrusted his own mother, they says. Well,
his mother, she'd had seventeen kids, not countin'm,
so they couldn' be much strength left in her. Ah!
a woman is always a woman, the bishop use' to
say. 'n she's the one that committed the first sin in
the Garden of Eden. Her man took a bite off the
apple only cause his wife gave it to him. Cause a
man is weak, you see, 'n he couldn' resist. It ain't
his fault; his wife had no business temptin him like
that, makin'm topple over into a life of sin. That's
why now she's punished 'n she must obey her man
who's the boss 'n the strongest. A man is only weak
when he's tempted by his wife, apart fr'm that, he's
always the strongest.

  ...Yep, women can't complain, cause it's their
own fault if it all started wrong. If only that first
woman could of kept still 'n not grab the damn
apple fr'm that tree. To lose the Garden of Eden fer
an apple!... Well, I got my own sayin that if the
woman pushed her man into doin som'n wrong,
well they must of been someone that pushed her too.
'n that it couldn'be all her fault. Cause they ain't a
woman I know that could let go her Paradise fer an
apple, now, no matter how juicy it is. 'n I don't see
why the first woman had to be any sillier than the
rest. Sometimes I say to myself that someone pushed
her; 'r else it was a trap; 'r that it had to happen
so that we could earn back our heaven by the sweat
of our brow. 'n in that case, I dunno why one person

should carry the blame instead of the next one. Cause they told us: it don't make no difference who would of been in Adam 'n Eve's place, they jus' would of done the same thing. It had to happen! A lotta times I ask myself why they gave us a Paradise, if it was settled all in advance we was supposed to lose it. Yep, how come they tempted us at all with their Paradise? We hadn' asked fer it. Ah! well, you see, we was destined to become sinners; 'n so you hadda have occasions fer sin. 'n it's Eve that started it all. 'n so now women, well... It's the bishop'mself that told us, 'n he's a saint, he is, he mus' know all about it.

'n then there was meat that we wasn' allowed to eat on Friday. Well, fer that matter, the Irish wasn' either. Fish on Friday was fer everybody... Everybody that could pay fer it, that is. Us, it wasn' too hard: along the coasts, there's more fish than meat. But my father use' to tell us we had kin livin inland, near Acadieville. 'n seems aroun' there it wasn' easy to find fish on Fridays. They was farmers 'n they could smoke'mselves a pig fer winter. But they was no herrin 'n no cod in'em places. So, they would eat bread 'n molasses to survive with salt pork on their conscience. But Gapi, he says that fish on Friday is a pretty good thing: it allows the poor fishermen to sell their oysters, their salmon 'n their lobster on the doorstep of some rich folks that don't wanna break up their Lent 'n their abstinence.

The thing I und'stand the least is on the one hand, the Good Lord says it ain't easy fer a rich man to go to heaven; but on the other hand, seems to me it ain't easy fer a rich man not to get there. A well-off man can respect all the church 'n the Lord's Commandments without goin through a great deal of trouble; he can pay his church dues, have his father 'n mother taken care of in their ol'age, buy fresh fish every Friday, get to church on Sunday 'n have a pew to sit in, 'n live his life with honour 'n respect without havin to steal 'r beat up his neighbour in order to make ends meet. A well-off man can have 'mself educated too, 'n an educated man, he don't swear 'n he don't blaspheme, he knows you shouldn' use the Lord's name in vain. He's also use'to workin, cause he ain't never short of a job, so he ain't lazy. Now you take a man that don't swear, that don't steal, that never skips mass, that takes care of his ol' father in his ol'age, 'n that ain't lazy... 'n try to make me und'stand how that man can manage not to go to heaven when he dies. Ain't a damn sin left fer him to catch. Lord knows, some people jus'ain't free to miss Paradise: they is destined to it since they was born.

Don't you find destiny is kind of a funny thing? What do you think it really is? Some says a person comes to life with heaven 'r hell already in his veins. If that's true, we'd be in a hell of a fix. We could be breakin our backs each day of our lives all we wanned... True, we don't seem to manage abidin by all the Commandments at once. If we keep one, we break another: it's hard to take care of yer ol'folks without runnin through other people's be-longin's: 'r to stop workin on Sundays 'n pay yer church dues at the same time. Lord knows, a down-'n-out man that stands firm by his Commandments, it's almos' like havin a cripple turnin somersaults over an electric wire.

But the thoughest thing is to be charitable: to give food to those that is hungry, clothes to those that ain't got none, 'n to go to prison to cheer up those that is inside. When a person has spent the week in prison, he don't feel like goin back in fer a Sunday visit. He don't feel like givin away his clothes 'r his bread 'n butter to som'one that don't need it more than him. Ain't easy fer a poor man to be charitable 'r to give to church. Which means he ain't never sure about his Salvation like the one that is better off, 'n can pay fer it cash.

Gapi, he says that if Paradise is only fer the rich folks, he'd rather not have anythin to do with it. An eternity you can buy, he says, sounds too much like this world of ours, 'n he's had enough with one. He ain't easy to deal with, Gapi, 'n when he gets boilin mad, he could jus' as well set Paradise on fire with hell's own flames. But it's no use gettin mad, I says to'm, 'r tryin to cheat, 'r even sulk in a corner 'n swear you're never gonna go nowhere. Once you're dead, it ain't over yet, you still gotta settle down somewhere. I told this to Gapi: you can't keep on standin there lik'a lamp-post, right at the gate of life 'n death, 'r even at the gate of heaven 'n hell. It'll have to be one 'r the other, 'n you won't be able to make yer choice. It'll already have been made, cause now is when you decide.

Ah! I know you ain't the only one to decide, but you also have som'n to say about it... You don't have much to say, but you sure as hell have a little som'n to say... You can always try anyway... You can try 'n say som'n... 'r else you can try not to do not'n wrong. Cause I already heard the priests sayin that whatever evil you may do, it's you alone that does it, nobody else helps you, 'n that's how come yer sins belong to you. But as fer yer charitable work, it's the Good Lord that makes you do it, 'n it belongs to him. So what it all means is that the only thing you can work out on yer own, is yer damnation; 'n if you wanna work out yer own salvation, the Good Lord has to be involved. 'n they also says that the Good Lord, who's infinitively perfect, is free, to be 'r not to be involved. That's why we end up not bein too sure about what we have to do in this matter, 'n we don't really know how to go about havin the Good Lord on our side. Specially since we ain't got the means to follow all that's recommended in the Commandments, the theological virtues, 'n the acts of mercy, spiritual 'n otherwise. We barely make it each time we manage to feed everybody we have in the house, 'n warm up their feet in our hands at night, so they can fall asleep before daybreak. We barely have time to fall on our knees, by our beds, 'n try to remember our prayers...

...Well, when I don't remember what comes after: "Pray fer us sinners 'n give us this day our daily bread"... I say whatever comes to my mind with words the Good Lord can und'stand. But more often than not, I don't say not'n at all, cause of my scrubber's knees that can't stand much kneelin. I end up sayin to the Good Lord not to depend on me too much, but to give me the grace to depend on Him, Amen. It ain't a prayer you can find in the holy books 'n I wouldn' try to say it in church; but at our place, kneelin by the stove, I figure that between the two of us, maybe the Good Lord isn' so infinitively fussy.

XII

THE CARDS

You gotta shuffle, cut, make a wish. That's it. Cut twice. Any wish you want, that's yer own business. Yer wish, you got it?... Okay. Now we're gonna see what life gave you 'n what it has in store fer you.

... Yep... Well now!

Might as well take off yer coat, you could get hot. Make yerself comfortable. 'n don't you fret 'r worry about not'n. The cards is gonna tell you the truth, that's fer sure; the only thing is, the truth has many faces, like my father use' to say. Sometimes, it's hard to know what truth means. Me, I can't tell you not'n more than the truth... Why don't you hang up yer coat right here, on the nail, 'n make yerself comfortable... Take the little pedlar, him, he worries about his cards. Every time he passes by, he wants to have his fortune told. 'n each time his fortune tells'm that luck is right behind'm. That didn' stop'm fr'm losin his job, his wife 'n his truck. Whenever he complains, I tell'm: Now, about the truck, it's a real pity, but a job 'n a wife that make you work so hard, maybe you're better off havin lost them somewhere. But him, he says like this that if luck does follow'm, it mus' be mighty far behind.

Well you, it's a jack of diamonds that's followin you. A jack of diamonds closely followed by a club with blue eyes, a white face 'n black hair. A club 'n a diamond. You'll hafta make a choice. Whenever you reach a point where life forks 'n you hafta make a choice, that's the toughest thing. If you could only know... but you can never know. A person never knows in advance what's in store fer'm in the end. At all costs, he wants to pick his life's happiness, at all costs. But it can happen just as easy as not that he'll pass right by it.

But I reckon it ain't as bad as havin no choice at all. When yer life is all mapped out in advance, 'n you're bound to follow it by hangin on to its petticoat, it ain't easy. Me, I says if a person's got no choice, it's almost like he's got no freedom at all. I figure a person is still better off facin a bad choice than a forced freedom. Like my mother use' to say: you're born cause you can't do otherwise, you're raised with all yer obligations in mind, you get married cause you have to, you're forced to live out the rest of yer life, 'n you know fr'm the start you'll perform yer last obligation with yer last breath... Well, that's what I call havin a forced freedom, all right.

Take the earth, fer instance. You're born on it, but it don't belong to you. You may feel like sayin this is yer home, 'n earth is as much yer own as it is to others, 'n you're gonna walk on it, straight ahead... won't be long you'll bang yer head against a fence 'r a post where it says: "NO TRESPASSIN". 'n so, you turn back cause you realize the earth ain't yours either. Me, I und'stand that Tim's house ain't mine, I mean it was Tim that built it in the first place; 'n *Elie*'s boat belongs to *Elie*, that's fair; 'n *Jude*'s truck is his, he paid fer it. But the earth, who paid fer it, 'n who made it? Who does it belong to in the first place? Ain't it to the Good Lord? 'n how the hell did it now come to belong to one person instead of another? Did some folk inherit the earth, fr'm father to son? Would the Good Lord 'mself have given it away to someone on his death bed?... Ah! well, here I am blasphemin. If it was Gapi talkin like that I'd make'm shut up. I'd say to'm that the Good Lord is just, 'n that it ain't him that gave away the earth to nobody, but that someone grabbed it, without askin'm. 'n that person left it to his descendants that split it up between 'emselves, lot by lot. 'n now, a person ain't free to go 'n take it away fr'm them.

That darn jack of diamonds is still after you. Watch out fer him. It's better to have too much than not enough. But still, keep an eye on the side of that club. He's waitin fer you at each turn of yer life, 'n you can rely on'm. I sure would. Yer joys, yer hopes 'n yer life's happiness is in clubs. Take good care of it. Yer life's happiness, if often comes when you didn' ask fer it, 'n also when you don't expect it. But you gotta take good care of it, cause it can go back where it came fr'm, without warnin you. Life is kind of strange, ain't it? Everybody's lookin fer his own happiness, no doubt about it. But how come it is some folks find it 'n some folks don't? Some men never got heart problems 'r lung diseases, 'n some women never had a single incurettage; 'n some folks ain't never had their feet cold either, 'r never heard their guts screamin or their kids howlin. I know some folks that can't even tell how deep a hole in a graveyard is. They had it all pretty easy, 'em ones.

...Had it all, that's a manner of speakin. Cause seems they still ain't happy. Ain't easy to make everybody happy: those that don't got not'n, want som'n; 'n those that got som'n, want more. Ain't easy. Well, I got a sayin of my own, that as long as a person can't have it all, he might as well not have too much. So that way, he can still be hopin fer som'n. Cause the worst problem that can hit a person, seems to me, it's to drink when he ain't thirsty, to eat when he ain't hungry 'r to sleep when he don't feel like it. That's the worst thing of all: to wish fer not'n no more, cause you already got everythin a person can have. That's the worst thing, 'n the way I see it, a person's better off not eatin his fill, so he can still find room to wish fer life's happiness.

As fer you, you have it, yer life's happiness. It's passin by right now, not far fr'm here. But I can't figure out of what kind of riches it's made of. It'll be between the diamonds 'n the clubs, but it's kind of funny... Yep... you got yer wish, you can thank the Lord fer it. You got it jus' the way you wanned it, samely 'n exactly. There's only one thing I don't und'stand: you got yer wish, but you don't know you got it. That's funny, cause usually, when a person's got his wish, he can figure out when he's got it. Not you... Darn it! Even though I been tellin fortunes all my life, unless you're wishin fer heaven after death, I can't figure out not'n about that wish of yours. I reckon you must of wished fer som'n rare that can't be found aroun' here. Oh! well... that's yer business, 'n I sure won't ask you to reveal yer wish.

...Usually, I sort of manage figurin out what everybody's wishin fer. To this day, I never seen *Elie* hopin to get a job; 'r *Zélica à Tilmon*, five times a widow, wishin 'rself a vocation. The young ones, well, they make wishes like all hell broke loose.

They'd like to be *Jean Béliveau* 'r our Holy Father
the Pope if they wasn' afraid of bein laughed at.
They jus' can't be satisfied with a small happiness,
at that age, a small happiness that would last fer a
while. No sir, they gotta have it all right away:
money, fancy clothes, the ol' countries, motorcycles,
Chryslers with an open top, four doors, white tires,
yellow lights, a fox-tail, 'n a backside that scrapes
the paved road. They see things in a big way, young
folks. But when a person's life starts wearin thin,
he und'stands a little better that you can't have it
all. Except if that person ain't fr'm aroun' here.
Ah! if you go to the States 'r to Ontario, things is
different. But over here, a person that's been married fer a while, 'n already raisin a family, 'n that's
been goin on stamps fer a number of years, well,
that person's wishes are kind of lanky. He'll be
hopin to win once at bingo, 'r see his children
make their grades, 'r find on some counter remnants
of calicoes 'n flannelettes to make new clothes outta
them. 'n then, when you get old, the only thing you
wish is fer yer last years to grow longer without
you botherin no one, 'n when yer time is up, to die
without passin away.

   Me... now ain't that funny... I only wished fer
one thing durin all my bloody life. Yep... all my life
I wished to own a house. Cause you can't call this
shack here a house. Takes in water, cold 'n wind,
it does... shakes in winter, sweats in summer... 'n
damn it! It just about falls over yer head each
Spring. Gapi can't bank it proper in the Fall cause
it leans too much to the South. I can't bring my
wash-tub inside cause I can't find no room on the
floor to stand it up; 'n I could hardly lay it on the
bed. So, I do my washin outside, winter 'r summer.
Ah! let me tell you this, between Advent 'n Candle-

mas day, we don't change our socks 'n our underwear too often... Nope, me, I never asked fer money.
Just a house. Ah! not a castle 'r a bungalow; just
a common enough house where I could do all my
chores inside; the washin, the ironin, the cookin,
'n also the raisin of children, everythin inside. Funny, ain't it? Cause I heard nowadays some women
only want one thing: to leave the house. Jus' when
they have everythin inside, that's when they wanna
leave. Maybe that's what would of happened to me
too, hard to say! I reckon a person gets bored of
everythin. Even of feelin good. Ah! yep... It's like I
says to Gapi sometimes: 'em ones that is tired of
feelin good should come 'n wash my load of dirty
clothes outside my door when it's five below zero;
'n try to bring in my full line of hand-towels 'n
underwear when they're frozen so hard they start
lookin like a bunch of ghosts fr'm *Richibuctou*; 'n
eat warmed up beans 'n pancakes; 'n get outta bed
aroun' four in the mornin to shove twigs 'n kindlin's
in a woodstove... I reckon everybody's gotta live
out his life 'n his destiny, 'n die when his hour has
come.

...We have a final hour 'n a life, 'n we gotta go
through with'em both. Looks like that's our destiny.
I reckon it's done on purpose. I ain't too sure who
dunnit, but it sure looks like we can't choose our
own life anymore than we can choose our own hour.
Some folks called it our book of life: they says Saint
Peter has a kind of big book where all our lives is
written down in advance with our dates of birth 'n
our death anniversaries. We can't go against destiny,
'r push back that final hour one notch, that's fer
sure... Maybe that's what the cards is tellin us.

Gapi says that it ain't true; nobody has decided
fr'm the start what he was goin to do later on. Ah!

I reckon that with Gapi, it ain't the same: they won't make'm do som'n against his will, Gapi. He's too hard-headed. 'n if he made up his mind not to go through a certain place, they won't convince'm, I know'm. But when his hour comes, he'll jus' have to go through with it, like everybody else... Well, wouldn' he have his hour, like the rest of us? Ah! Gapi... a person can't really know what they're gonna do with'm, once he gets there. He says that he's free, yep, 'n nobody'll dare to bother him none. Destiny, he don't believe in that.

...He says to me the other day: not'n is written down, 'n a man decides his life, step by step. This minute, I'm free, he says, to go to shore 'n relieve myself if I want to, right now, 'n that ain't written in no book, he says. Well... maybe it ain't written down in no book, but, Gapi 'r no Gapi, I ain't too sure he can stop fr'm relievin nature when he's got the urge. So I wouldn' take the risk of floutin destiny too much.

...Ah! as fer you, you're in clubs way over yer head, but you can't let go óf the diamonds. Cause there's a jack followin you. I think there comes a time when a person's gotta make up his mind. Seems to me that the time has come fer you to make a decision. I ain't the one that's tellin you this, it's the cards. It's 'em diamonds 'n clubs. Yer wish 'n yer life's happiness, you got'em. But I'm pretty sure one of these days, you're gonna have to make a choice. Maybe it's som'n that has to do with a job? 'r a line of life? You know, sometimes the cards ain't much clearer than the soapy water in my bucket. When a ten of hearts pops in right between yer club 'n yer diamond, the waters get troubled, that's fer sure. But don't you worry: 'cordin to what

I see, you jus' hit a mine. Good God, it's like you found a treasure! Maybe it ain't a treasure in money... looks to me like it's som'n else... like a... ah! ain't easy to figure out yer cards, you... Holy Mother of our Father in Heaven!... if it wasn' jus' about like blasphemin... I'd say yer wish 'n yer life's happiness ain't too far fr'm here. There's som'n wrong, damn it! Cause yer wish comes true, 'n it's som'n good, 'n like I said, looks like a real treasure to me... but it's right aroun' here... I'm almos' sittin on it, damn it! Jesus Christ! Could it be by any chance that you been wishin to shove yer head in my bucket?

...Forgiv'em. When you been fortune-tellin with'em cards fer a long time, a person ends up seein only jacks, queens, 'n kings, 'n also ends up forgettin the respect that is due to you. You'd better shuffle them again.

...You gotta shuffle, cut, make a wish. That's it. Cut twice. Any wish you want, that's yer own business. Yer wish, you got it?... Okay, now we're gonna see what life gave you 'n what it has in store fer you.

... A jack of diamonds 'n clubs... damn it!

XIII

_____ SPRING

Ah! well, Holy Mother of Christ! will you look at that this mornin! Gapi! Come 'n see, Gapi! Ain't no less than ten regiments of wild geese in the sky, this mornin. 'n not a speck of snow on the roofs. Makes you feel good to fill up yer lungs with fresh air early in the mornin. April can't be far away now. Gapi! Is the month of March over yet?... Should be soon. Mus'be Spring these days, fer sure. If only they hadn' taken my calendars. Had the Arvin's one, 'n the one of l'Aratouère, 'n of the Royal Canadian Mounting Police. But there's always aroun' some kid that takes'em fr'm me, cause of the picture... Is the month of March over, Gapi? That's the least of Gapi's worries, what day of the week it is, or what month of the year. He says it ain't cause we got a calendar that we're closer or farther fr'm death; or that we ain't gonna stop the time jus' cause we can give it a name. Maybe we ain't gonna stop it, but we sure can look at it passin by, 'n know that some times is better than others.

Got a sayin of my own, that Spring is the good season fer us. Some say it's summer. But I'm pretty sure that to be happy, a person's gotta hope fer som'n, som'n better. So, durin the whole of Spring, we're hopin fer summer. We wait fer clams 'n quahaugs, fer blueberries 'n warm weather, 'n fer'em picnics at Sainte-Anne's 'n Sainte-Marie's. While in the month of August, we ain't waitin fer not'n anymore. It ain't havin som'n that gets a person feelin good, it's knowin you're gonna have it. That's why Spring is the best of times, I says.

I remember the days when I stayed at my father's, 'n when my mother was still alive. We had us a small piece of land aroun' the house. Ah! not a big farm 'n no lumber land either. Jus' half a field of clover that he'd wanna plough once every five years. In'em years, my mother would hurry 'n plant her gardenin seeds over three or four rows, before my father had time to turn'em into oat fields. 'n then, she'd send us to weed'em. 'n all the time we was weedin, we was thinkin of the month of July with its turnips 'n its carrots, 'n the month of August with'em corn-cobs. We wasn' thinkin 'bout flies 'n mosquitoes, right then, or 'bout crows 'n hail. In Spring, you never think of mosquitoes 'n crows. But you watch the wild geese go by 'n you fill yer lungs with fresh air. 'n you wait.

Gapi says, makes a person moody to keep on hopin like that. We're better off not gettin any ideas, he says, if we don't wanna be disappointed. Says that a person 'd never feel hurt if he hadn' started believin in dreams. All right, all right, I says. Musn' build dreams. Musn' build castles, I says to him. But we can always wait fer the month of July, cause we're pretty sure 'bout that... Ain't we sure 'bout that? I says to him. We ain't never sure 'bout not'n, he says, 'n you can't believe in'em dreams. So, you know you can't count on Gapi to change yer tune cause yer changin seasons. He don't put his trust in Spring anymore than he puts it in priests, in oysters, or in the gov'ment. Says he don't trust nobody to live his life for him. Fer that matter, couldn' of trust 'mself either, cause his life, well... Ain't easy when you ain't got a trade, an education, or nobody to get you out of the hole. Gapi says he don't want nobody's help; well, that's cause he knows even if he wanned some, he wouldn' get none... Ain't easy.

'n yet, he ain't lazy, Gapi. In any case, when he's workin, he's on his feet. 'n the day he came by, his hatchet on his shoulder, lookin fer me at my father's place, — that was more than fifty years ago — well, he wasn' sittin on his butt, I'm tellin you. Young 'n sturdy, he was. 'n his shoulders was stronger than a moose, that's right! He stood straight, in those days, with his hair real black 'n his eyes like the blue sea. 'n he had all his teeth, 'n hair on his chest. It was Spring, like today. The wild geese was comin'in fr'm the South; 'n the seagulls was so crazy they'd throw 'mselves against the masts 'n get caught in the sails. They was already some pine-cones on the trees, almost as big as that, 'n the sap was drippin fr'm the branches. The air 'n the earth that day was smellin so good, that even if Gapi had stunk, I think I wouldn' of noticed, I'm tellin you.

Well, summer passed; 'n autumn came with its rottin soil, 'n winter with ice over the bay 'n wind through the cracks of the house. Those days, I couldn' do my washin no more, without the clothes freezin hard on the line; 'n Gapi started stinkin, like the others. But when Spring started to wake up fr'm its winterin, we all decided to come out, 'n we got back our strength. 'n the air started smellin like perfume, 'n Gapi too, I'm tellin you!... Well, almost. Almost as much as the year before. But the followin year, Spring came late, 'n we had to bury a new-born child. So, that season, I figured summer had hooked on to winter, 'n they hadn' been any month of April. Even the wild geese wasn' flyin over no more, 'n they was no May flowers to be found. You could of said it was a Spring squeezed in between ice-packs 'n fire-flies. No wild geese, that year, 'n no musk in the woods, 'n Gapi didn' smell too good either.

Well, it went away, like the rest. Bad times always end up passin. They pass like rancid butter when you spread it between two slices of bread. Best thing is to close yer eyes 'n wait fer better times. You can stay with yer eyes shut fer a long while; but every now 'n then, there comes a Spring with wild geese 'n pine-cones. 'n it's jus' like I says to Gapi: after you fasted all through Lent, you find that baloney 'n hard boiled eggs sure taste good on Easter mornin.

...You see, maybe Spring is a gift the Good Lord gives to poor folks alone, since you must of been shiverin jus' about all winter to be wishin so hard fer April's sun; 'n you must of been buried in snow to go out with yer hatchet 'n dig yerself some water furrows; 'n you must of been eatin warmed-up beans fer months in a row, to come out 'n smell the fresh air 'n think 'bout 'em small early carrots still asleep underground. Spring is made fer those folks that had a tough time gettin through winter. That's how come I says it's the season of the ol' folks or of the poor folks.

I says like this, that a person's got a season of his own, like he's got his destiny 'n his final hour. When yer time comes, you gotta give up; you can grumble, 'n kick, 'n get yer back up, but you're gonna go anyway. You also gotta live through yer fate; that's in writin 'n you can't erase it. Well, same thing with the seasons 'n the months of the year. You can't help it. It's cause of the water, 'n the sun, 'n the smell of the woods that gets under yer skin. Ain't only a question of findin som'n to eat. I try to tell Gapi 'bout it. Why is it the salmons come back swimmin up-stream? Why is it the wild geese fly home against the wind? Makes you think, don't it? It means there's som'n in this life-givin earth that looks like you or ties you down.

Yet, that's gotta be why you stay on this earth, cause it looks like you. A person is a little bit like a tree or an animal: he ends up wearin the colour of the earth that fed him. Take the rabbits in the woods, they is white in winter, 'n grey in summer; that's how come they manage not to get caught: they look too much like the green 'r the snow. I think that's why we too end up lookin pretty much like the earth.

Our skin is kind of brown 'n a little bit cracked; 'n as we grow ol', the wrinkles of the face look like furrows in a garden; 'n bones get crooked at the joints like branches of a birch tree; 'n feet sink into the earth like they wanned to take root. We look like this land, I'm tellin you.

This land, 'n the sea. She's the one that fed us most 'n saved us fr'm distress. When the land happens to fail you, you still got the sea, with its clams 'n its smelts. Shouldn' speak ill of the sea, I says to the others, she saved us so many many times. Even if high tides in Fall come 'n get you right up to yer kitchen floor; 'n the ice in Spring takes yer boat at sea; 'n storms on the other side of the sand dunes drown fishermen every year. Even then, she's the one that made us, 'n looks like us the most.

Usin her as a mirror, our eyes turned deep 'n blue. 'n havin watched so long fer fish deep in the water, our cheeks rose high 'n our brows grew close. That's why we end up lookin like the sea that surrounds the country. Yep, that's what they says. They says we got a low 'n raspy voice. Maybe true. 'n that we don't talk fast. Well, we ain't use' to talkin a lot cause we don't know too much what to say to people. So, when strangers come around, we hold our tongue. Not that we ain't got not'n to say, we'd like to tell'em 'bout the sea, 'n the country, 'n us... But usually, we only ask'em 'bout their folks 'n their jobs. 'n at the end, well... Ain't easy talkin to people, with a raspy voice.

Well, I think we've been breathin too long the salt of the water, 'n it stayed stuck in the throat; 'n the nor'easter widened our foreheads; 'n the pebbles hardened the soles of our feet; 'n the cry of the gulls in the sou'wester 'n the wail of the wave that comes crashin on the sand-banks at night got entangled in our ears, 'n that's why we don't talk fast 'n why our voice kind of drawls, like they say.

Well, a person's gotta take 'mself for what he is, 'n not try to talk 'n walk like other folks. When you 'n yer forefathers have been walkin fer two centuries on rows of red soil, or on pebbles 'n shells, you can't have wobbly legs 'n springs in yer feet; 'n when you've been forced to face the winds of the open sea, you jus' can't have skin that's white 'n soft; 'n how can you talk fancy with all that sea salt in yer lungs 'n throat?... Nope, a person's gotta look like the land that made him 'n fed him, 'n that's what ties him up at home 'n makes him ache. 'n wakes up in Spring, it does. 'n it makes you remember...

Funny, but me, Spring, it makes me wanna go out 'n whistle, 'n walk faster than usual; but it also makes me ache. Hard to explain. Like if I had a cork jammed between the heart 'n the tonsils, or cotton-wool where the lungs is. It ain't a heart-ache, not'n like that. Nope... It's like an achin, but not an achin 'bout som'one or som'n... more like an achin fer the sun... way back then.

...The snow would start meltin in March, half through Lent. The other kids, to keep Lent, they wouldn' eat no sugar 'n no chocolate. So us, to try 'n do the same, we'd save the orange we had fer Christmas, 'n we'd leave it there on top of the cupboard till Easter, as penance. 'n on Easter Saturday, on the stroke of the Angelus, we'd jump on the orange: well, it was rotten. We'd lost an orange, but we'd saved our Lent, 'n we was happy. 'n durin the whole month of April, we'd gather small tadpoles fr'm the brooks 'n we'd watch'em turn into frogs inside the bottles; then, we'd let'em go. 'n in the month of May, we'd walk three miles every night to do our prayers fer the *mois de Marie*. It ain't that we had to do it, but it made us go across the baseball field; so we'd stop there fer a while to watch'em play. 'n already in the month of June, they was rhubarb at our neighbour's, 'n all the women was plantin, 'n weedin, 'n callin'mselves names fr'm one fence to the other. Funny, but each Spring, it all comes back to me, 'n it makes me ache.

...Makes me ache, but it ain't a sad ache. Nope. More like if... All right, just imagine you're out on yer door-step, one Spring mornin, 'n you see wild geese passin over 'n goin inland, behind yer father's place, right where you was born 'n where you was raised. 'n you see a drop of water clingin

to the tip of a branch, 'n then you hear it fall on
the snow, 'n run in the furrow, 'n rush to the shore,
into the sea. 'n you can jus' feel the clover that 'd
like to come out of the earth, 'n the ice goin down
the river. 'n the seagulls cryin after the wild geese,
'n the wild geese still flyin north... 'n you don't
know where you are no more. You start hearin the
cries of the tadpoles, the songs of the *mois de Marie*,
'n the crackin of the ice all along the bay. Its like
yer life is all bunched up in yer veins 'n you can
no longer tell the difference between sunny days
of the past 'n the ones of today, or between the
gulls' cryin 'n yer neighbours' name-callin. Like all
yer memories come rushin back, while Spring closes
in, 'n you look at the passin of the wild geese. All
yer memories, all yer hopes, 'n all yer achin. You
feel like whistlin, 'n diddlin... but you can't cause
you got that cork right here 'n cotton-wool where the
lungs is...

But one day, maybe we'll find a Spring season,
a real one, drippin all over 'n reekin of musk, with
endless processions of wild geese in the sky, 'n no
more achin, just a nice easy feelin in yer throat
'n all over the skin, a real Spring that'll never end,
but that'll last, 'n last, 'n... well, that'll be heaven, 'n
that day, gotta feelin we'll all be dead and in Paradise.
Gonna go 'n see if *la Sainte's* got a calendar.

XIV

————————THE RISURRECTION

Gapi, he don't wanna believe the Good Lord came back to life on Easter mornin. Says it can't be done. When a man is dead, he says, he's dead. Maybe a man, I says to him: but the Good Lord ain't a man. He ain't a man? he says; well, if He ain't man, how come He died? 'n that's when I tol'm to quit blasphemin.

...How come He died?... They told us it was to resurrect better. But why is it He resurrected? Could it really be cause He wanned to stay with us all the time? Ah! I can und'stand He'd wanna stay with us, but... but I don't und'stand it. Fer a person so dead sure of findin Salvation, like the Good Lord is, I sure don't see what could be keepin'm around here. If I'd been in His place, it so happens... yep, well it so happens I wasn' in His place.

We can't be in His place, none of us. Well, not *la Sagouine*, anyway. All of that holy stuff, it ain't a job fer me. Seems to me that spendin my life surrounded by angels, popes, cardinals, 'n Holy sees, seems to me I wouldn' feel comfortable. 'n a person jus' can't be gettin only the honours, fer a job like that, he's gotta be able to do the works. 'n the Good Lord's work, I figure it's one helluva job. Specially nowadays. In the ol' days, maybe it was okay. But today, to try 'n rule the world 'n control the peoples' minds, except fer our priest, I don't see nobody else to do it but the Good Lord 'mself.

Ah! It ain't that I believe He don't know what He's doin. I'm sure the Good Lord knows His stuff. He knows all right, He knows that if you got Rollefellers 'n Rolleroyces rollin in money, it's fer the greater glory of God 'n fer our own good too. Us, we don't know what's our own good anyway. How can we know what's in His mind when the high tides come up 'n flood our kitchen floors! But that don't mean there's som'n wrong with His mind, jus' cause we can't und'stand it. Maybe without'em high tides that year, we wouldn' have any smelts the next one. 'n without depression 'r financial crash, we wouldn' of had soup 'n stamps. 'n would we have had our widow's compensation if our men hadn' died at war? Sure gives Him a lotta things to think about, to the one that's rulin the world. 'n I think some days He must have a headache 'r two, the poor devil. Some days He mus'be almost sorry fer havin made such a world at all. Cause He very well could of decided not to make it. 'r He could of done it different...

That's what Gapi told me one day. He says like this: If the Good Lord wasn' bound to make this world of ours, He was even less bound to make it the way He did. What was the big idea, he says, makin potato bugs 'n givin wings to crows? 'n why the hell did He have to create ninety mile an hour winds on the very same day He made waves seventy feet high?... I dunno what kind of world Gapi would of made... I dunno fer sure...

...What kind of world all of us would of made in His place... If it's true we're all gonna risurrect, us too, well seems to me we'll be able to remake this world of ours the way we like it. Like the Creator that made it in His own image 'n resemblance, on the very first day. I think if I tried to make it in

my own image, wouldn' be no great loss; but in my
own resemblance... If the resurrected folks started
lookin like what's in my bucket... might as well not
go through all the trouble of bringin'em up fr'm
their graves. Cause Him, after three days, they did
bring'm up fr'm His grave. Me, sure won't be after
three days; I'll have to wait fer my turn at the end
of time, after the Last Judgment. Sure wish that
p'ticular day was behind me. I dunno no one that's
yearnin fer his Last Judgment. Except fer *la Sainte*
that thinks she's better than the others. But when
they gonna start spellin out her past sins in front of
everyone, maybe she won't feel like such a saint
after all... Well, fer that matter, me neither. When I
think about that day, I'm almost sorry I didn' make
a nun.

Ah! sure's good to know though, the minute the
Last Judgment's over, right then we're gonna resurrect. Now, does that mean we're gonna come back
the way we is now, 'n as ol' as when we died? 'n if
I pass away at ninety, am I gonna be draggin out'em
ninety years fer all eternity? 'n the hunchback, is he
gonna have his hump? 'n ol' *Monique* her dead eye?
They says we'll be perfectly happy. If that's so, they
better give her eye back to *Monique*, 'n straighten
out the hunchback. They also gonna have to rub my
skin, 'n drain the water fr'm my knees. As fer Gapi,
it'll take a whole regiment of Archangels to put'm on
his feet again. Cause be won't be happy with only
his two arms 'n his thirty-six teeth, Gapi. I know'm:
he'll want som'n nobody ever saw, 'r som'n bigger
than the others... never happy, Gapi. 'n I pity the
Good Lord that's gonna try 'n resurrect that man.

Ah! well, the're still gonna resurrect'm like the
others, they can't leave Gapi alone in the graveyards

after the Last Judgment. That day, everybody's gonna
have to go through with it: through judgment 'n
through risurrection. Big 'n small, rich 'n poor alike.
Fer the poor folks, they won't be no great fuss:
can't be worse off than before; won't be able to
risurrect'em poorer than what they was. But rich
folks, fer them, it ain't guaranteed risurrection is
gonna be such a good thing. What if *Dominique à
Pierre* comes out of his grave plumb naked, with
not even a trouser-pocket to carry his wallet? What
would be have left, *Dominique*, without his wallet?
'n if they ain't no more judgments after the Last
Judgment, what are they gonna do with all of them
judges 'n lawyers? 'n what will they do with the
doctors if they ain't no sick people any more? Fer
that matter, I dunno what'll they do with me neither,
cause up there, I can't believe they'll still be needin
their floors scrubbed! Oh well, I'll let my ol'bones
have a rest.

   ...An eternity, it can be a long while, fer a rest.
Seems they is not'n in this world that comes near to
bein that long. At the Mission, they was a priest fr'm
a far away country, 'n he use' to tell us if the wing of
a bird brushed lightly on a rock once every one
hundred years, well by the time the rock was worn
out, eternity would jus' be startin... but it couldn' be
a bird fr'm around here, cause the ones I know
would of died 'fore wearin out the rock. That priest
fr'm the Mission, he also use' to say they was no
danger of gettin bored durin that eternity, cause we'd
spend our time listenin to the song of the skylarks 'n
enjoyin the sweet-smellin flowers of Paradise. That's
what he says, 'n he's a priest, he must know what
he's talkin about. He also says we'd all have a white
gown 'n a candle. Well, that's when Gapi gave a
straight "nope". Tried all I could to 'splain to'm he

could keep his overalls under his gown if he wanned,
no way. He says he'd rather not risurrect at all.

     Poor Gapi! It's easy to see he don't und'stand
not'n to mysteries. I says to him: open up a little 'n
try to und'stand. Except it ain't easy und'standin risurrection when you ain't got no education. Fer the
priests 'n the lawyers, a mystery is as plain as day-
light... But fer us... the only thing they taught us,
it's that a mystery is a truth that you gotta believe in,
but that you don't und'stand. Now try 'n und'stand
som'n after that! I und'stand that I'm gonna die, that
my body is gonna go to the graveyard, 'n my soul
to Pewgatory 'r to Heaven... But little ol'me, *la Sagouine*, where the hell am I gonna be durin all that
time? They says that when Risurrection comes, my
soul is gonna rejoin my body, 'n I'll turn back into
what I was before. But, don't forget, that's on Last
Judgment day; at the end of time. Well, am I gonna
stay split in two until the end of time? 'n what do I
know, if time has it in its mind to end soon? 'n me,
what'll I do in the meantime? That's what's been
runnin through my head 'n buggin me no end.

     ...I always have a bunch of ideas runnin through
my head, fer that matter. On risurrection 'n on eternity. When they says the Good Lord made us, 'n
made the earth, 'n all the things that grew on it, well
then I ask myself, who could of made Him? So then
they says nobody made Him, He made Himself; He
made Himself eternally. There He was, the Good
Lord, fer all eternity, by Himself. Well, not all by
Himself: with His three persons in God. Lucky thing
they was three... wasn' borin that way. Cause it
makes no difference how far back a person goes,
He was already there. So then you say to yerself:
well before He was already there, what was there?

Nope, He was there. Before He arrived, He'd already come. That's what eternity is all about, they told us.

Yeah... Ah! course I know the people alone couldn' mak'emselves, that som'one hadda be there to bring'em out of not'n. 'n that's the Good Lord. But how come fer Him, they was no one to bring Him out of not'n? Sometimes I says to myself it must be as hard fer a Good Lord to come out of not'n as it is fer the people alone to mak'emselves... Well, here I am just like Gapi, blasphemin against the three persons in God.

...I believe in God, the Father Almighty, and in Jesus Christ His only Son our Lord, who was conceived fr'm the Holy Ghost... the Holy Ghost... He's the one, the Holy Ghost, that turned'mself into a firefly on Pentecost to fall on the heads of the apostles 'n giv'em the gift of tongues. Now the apostles, bein only fishermen lik'us, they came out of there all shaken up 'n started speakin seven tongues, imagine that, just like *Marguerite Michaud*. To make a fisherman speak seven tongues, don't make no difference what kind of fishin he does, that's a mystery that you don't und'stand too well, but that you gotta believe in, cause it's the Lord that revealed it.

Sure makes a lotta things to und'stand fer poor folks that haven' been in school very long, but that would still like to know in advance what's in store for'em on the other side. Cause if we could know a little bit of what's on the other side, maybe we could prepare 'rselves better so we don't get there lookin like dummies who ain't never seen not'n. We would sure like not to make the Good Lord 'n the Holy Virgin ashamed of us, on the day we'd enter Paradise at the end of time. We'd like to be ready lik'em others. 'n we sure wouldn' of minded havin a religion with a little bit less mystery 'n a little more holy bread on Easter mornin.

...But I better not think about that too much, cause it'll make me dizzy, like when I cross the railroad bridge 'n see the water underneath, between the track beams.

Gapi told me I was givin myself a lotta trouble fer not'n. That kind of thinkin, he told me, it drives a man straight to Saint John's; 'n to think too much about death only makes you croak faster. It ain't dyin that gets me thinkin, I says to'm, it's what comes after. What comes after death is death, he says. 'n I tol'm to quit blasphemin.

There's only one thing we know fer sure: 'n that's we're gonna go through it. I dunno where we'll go through, but we'll go through som'n. 'n if we come out of it, it'll be cause we're risurrected. 'n then, seems we'll be able to satisfy 'rselves to our hearts' content. Me, jus' to think about it brings to my mouth all the water I got in my knees. An eternity to reshape the world the way you want it! To take it in yer hands, 'n clean it up, 'n round it! 'n improve its looks, 'n... imagine! an eternity only fer you 'n yer risurrection alone!... Nope, not alone. Not all alone. With the Good Lord. But not only with the Good Lord either. With the others too.

...With *Joséphine*, 'n *Séraphine*, 'n *Pierre à Tom*, 'n *Elie*; 'n *Maxime* with his fiddle; 'n *Pierre Fou*, might as well. I think *Laurette à Johnny*'ll be there, 'n the late Johnny 'mself, fer that matter. Ah! well, with *Laurette*, I always managed to have my way. But not with *la Sainte*! With her, it can only mean an eternity of vespers, supplications 'n blessings of the Blessed Sacrament. 'n that's if she doesn' get into her head to start, on the other side, novenas of the Way of the Cross. If she's been suckin up to the Good Lord all her life, she sure ain't through on the other side. I still have in mind that big pot of stew she stole fr'm me, right on my own doorstep. Well that one, she won't take it back to Heaven. If she wants it real bad, she'll just have to take it... Oh!... I figure it can't bring you any luck to wish yer fellow man to go to hell fer a pot of stew. 'n I believe it ain't Christian. But I'm still gonna tell her to make a choice: she won't come with my stew. 'n she'll also have to give back to *la Cruche* her two *poutines*; 'n the fox-tail she stole fr'm *Noume*'s Ford to put it around her neck... Fer that matter, *Noume*'ll have to give back his beer to *Elie*, 'n *Elie* bring back to Gapi his spear 'n his rake... 'n I think I won't be able to keep *Séraphine's* shoes, 'n the Eaton catalogues I borrowed fr'm *la Sainte*. I kind of think a lotta folks are gonna have to give back a lotta things... Ah! after all, if *la Sainte* can stop plottin 'n meddlin in other people's business... I'll tell her she can come. But she'll be warned, she better not start makin any trouble. I only hope Gapi won't get into his head he ain't comin... I better go 'n talk to'm right now.

There's some things you can't delay settlin. You can wait a year to change the seaweed around yer shack, 'r fix the shingles on yer roof. Ain't no hurry either to wash the inside of yer cupboard 'n to air the blankets on yer clothes-line. But a person that puts off his salvation could be late fer his resurrection. Well me, I missed a lotta things in my life; I ain't about to miss this one. I'm gonna tell'm, Gapi. He don't wanna believe the Good Lord risurrected

on Easter mornin? Fine, I'm gonna say to'm: believe
it 'r don't believe it. Do it yer way. I'm gonna tell'm;
but don't you count on me, the mornin of Last
Judgment, to pull you out of yer grave 'n risurrect
you against yer will. Watch out you don't spend yer
eternity all by yerself: it could be longer than you
think, I'm gonna say to'm.

I'm gonna say it to him straight, right now.

XV

THE CENSUS

Sure 'nough, they came around fer the census. And don't you worry, they took a census of us all: they censed Gapi, and they censed *la Sainte*, and they censed me too. Ah! a big thing, it was, 'n you can take my word fer it that ain't never lied. See, when the're incensin, they gotta cense everybody, includin chickens 'n pigs. But us, we ain't got a chicken coop 'r a pigsty, so they went right along 'n censed the cats. They nose about yer clothes too, 'n they measure yer house 'n they even count the shingles on yer roof. But when they asked Gapi fer his bank-book, he told'em to shove it up their ass. Ah!... ain't got no manners, Gapi.

And they question you. Ain't always easy to answer: yer name, all yer Christian names, yer father, yer mother, yer terminal sickness, yer birthday, yer dead children, yer children still alive, 'n how much you make in a year. Gapi figured they was pryin too much in his life; so, when they asked him what was his father doin before he died, he took a good look at'em 'n says:

— *Fore dyin? My father stretched out both his legs 'n went: heug!*

Ah! tough things, they ask you.

Like a person would have to remember every damn' thing he did in his life. Good Lord! that's worse than goin to confession. They wanna know how much flour you use up in a year. One year, would you believe it! Now can you tell me if there's a single person in this world that knows how much flour he uses up in a year? We buy flour by the pound, a small bag atta time, when they ain't no more, 'n when we got the money; or when they let us have it on credit. And us, well, we make bread 'n pancakes with flour, 'n not account books, that's what Gapi told the censors. And we ain't got no book to write down every quahaug 'n clam that we sold. All we could tell the census was we go fishin to sell, we sell to buy, 'n we buy enough to fill up the stomach. 'n by the end of the year, they ain't no more fish in yer belly than what you caught in the bay. That's the way our economy goes.

Well, some of the questions are tougher to answer than others. Like when they asked *la Cruche* what she does fer a livin... or when they asked Boy à Polyte to give the names of all his children... ain't easy.

And they also ask you 'bout yer religion. So, you get yerself ready to answer, then you think it over. Cause, then too, you gotta come up with some explainin. Ain't all bein baptized 'n conformed by a real archbishop on a conformation tour. You gotta name the patron saint of yer actual parish. Now yer actual parish, is that the same one where you do yer Easter duties each Trinity Sunday? The parish where they baptize yer kids, is that an actual parish? Well, we sure didn' wanna look like communists, so we took a chance on tellin'em we was Christians.

That ain't all. Cause they got in their lists a question a lot tougher. Ah! there too, even Gapi didn' know what to answer. Yer nationality, they ask you. Citizenship 'n nationality. Hard to say.

...We live in America, but we ain't Americans. Nope, Americans, they work in'em factories in the States, and in summer, they come around, visitin our beaches in their white trousers 'n speakin English. 'n the're rich, them Americans, 'n we ain't. Us, we live in Canada; so we figure we mus' be Canadians.

...Well, that ain't true either, cause the Dysarts, 'n the Carrolls, 'n the Jones, they just ain't like us, and they also live in Canada. If the're Canadians, we sure can't be the same. Cause the're English, 'n us, we're French.

...Nope, we ain't completely French, can't say that: the French folks is the folks fr'm France, *les Français de France*. 'n fer that matter, we're even less *Français de France* than we're Americans. We're more like French Canadians, they told us.

Well, that ain't true either. French Canadians are those that live in *Québec*. They call'em *Canayens* or *Québécois*. But how can we be *Québécois* if we ain't livin in *Québec*? Fer the love of Christ, where do we live?

...In *Acadie*, we was told, 'n we're supposed to be *Acadjens*. So, that's the way we decided to answer the question 'bout nationality: *Acadjens* we says to them. Now then, we can be sure of one thing, we're the only ones to have that name. Well, them censors didn' wanna write down that word on their list. The way they sees it, seems *l'Acadie* ain't a country, 'n *Acadjen* ain't a nationality, cause of the fact it ain't written in Joe Graphy's books.

Well, after that we didn' know what else to say, 'n we told'em to give us the nationality they wanned. So, I think they put us down with the Injuns.

Ah! ain't easy earnin yer livin when you ain't got a country of your own, 'n when you can't tell yer nationality. Cause you end up not knowin what the hell you are. You feel like you're in the way, or like nobody wants you around any more. It ain't cause of what they tell you. Sure, they says you're a full-fledged citizen; but they can't name yer nationality. Maybe you ain't in the way, but you don't have yer place in the country. So, one by one, we'll all end up leavin one day or another.

I heard the saint's boy sent fer his mother. Yep, good ol' Arthur now, the one that settled in Montreal last summer. Seems he got a job, down there, in a plastic flower factory. 'n now, he sends fer his mother.

You can be sure she's gonna put on the feather hat she got fr'm the doctor's missus; 'n the foxtail she stole fr'm Noume's Ford. And if she's all dressed up like that, ain't no doubt she's gonna wear those Montreal side-walks down to the gravel. And at last, she's gonna light that church candle in *l'aratouère*, the big one dollar one, at the foot of *Frère André's* heart.

Yep, but here at least, ain't gonna be no trouble fer a while. If she can only stay long enough down there... Gapi says she won't come back... Really! ... Well... now, could that mean that...? Ah! Gapi, he always has to figure out the worst.

He also tells that Laurette à Johnny is gonna leave fer the States. 'n that Jos à Polyte is ready to

bring his family down South. That's what they've
been sayin at l'Orignal's place. Pretty soon, they
won't be a damn' neighbour to help you cast yer
boat. Rough times ahead, they says, 'n we could see
these parts once again censed, measured, turned
upside down 'n thrown down South.

We was already thrown out once, like that, 'n
fer sure, we landed in Louisiana. If it's gonna start
all over again!... Don't they think we had enough
already? My father use' to tell us his own grandfather
still had memories of that Expulsion, 'n he filled
their evenings with stories of those past miseries.
They walked fer days 'n months through the woods
to come back home, cause them also wanned to
have a country. They wanned to get 'mselves a patch
of land, where they could speak their own language,
'n where nobody could call'em names no more.
That's why they came back here, to their country, to
their lands. That's what they did, the ancestors of
my dead father. Well, seems they couldn' find'em
again, those lands of theirs: the English had taken
them all. Not'n left, they had, but a hatchet to cut
some trees 'n rebuild 'mselves. They built back their
houses, 'n started to live once more on the land of
their forefathers; but durin that Expulsion, they lost
their deeds 'n their nationality.

Ah! sure ain't easy to be deported like that, 'n
to think you ain't gonna get a couple of feathers
ruffled fer yer troubles. No free rides in'em trips.
True, they talk about you, after that: they give you
all sorts of nice names like *Evangéline* 'n *Les Saints
martyrs canadjens*. A heroic 'n martyred people, they
says, and they almost put you right up there with
the Holy Heart of Jesus. They was some people fr'm
L'Assomption Insurance Company 'n fr'm the Cathe-

dral that came to talk to us about that, in the basement of the church. They told us all about *l'Evangéline* 'n *l'Ave Marie-Stella*. Was a nice story, the one about *Marie-Stella* 'n *l'Evangéline*; still, I liked a lot more the stories of my late father.

...The story of Pierre à Pierre à Pierrot, dressed up like a woman, I'm tellin you, 'n that got away climbin up the trees, jumpin fr'm branch to branch like a monkey, so he wouldn' be seen by the Injuns 'n the English that was waitin fer him in the woods. Had to go 'n get some help fer the others that'd stayed behind, locked up in a cellar. An empty one, on top of that. 'n then, they was the story of captain Belliveau that was a prisoner with the others 'n was bein deported with'em. Well, that ol' captain threw all of the English overboard, 'n grabbed the helm. So there's a schooner that steered clear of Louisiana 'n never saw its shores. She anchored somewhere up North, my father use' to say, 'n the English never got wind of it. Seems our late forefathers wasn' easy to deal with, 'n you just couldn' pull the wool over their eyes. Well, it wasn' them, the heroes 'n the martyrs. Nope, the heroes 'n the martyrs was *Evangéline* 'n *Marie-Stella*.

Yep... we belong to the race of the holy martyrs, they told us, 'n seems we was lucky, bein expulsed like that. Ah! lucky we was, that's fer sure. First, they guaranteed us that almost half of the folks that was hoisted aboard the schooners, came back home. 'n of those that came round, almost half of them managed to rebuild their houses 'n get through the first winter. That was two hundred years ago, 'n there's still a lot of us around. The English 'mselves told us: after a storm like that one, most races would of come up with no survivors! You can count yerselves lucky, they says. Ah! fer that matter, we sure was lucky.

...It's been two hundred years, 'n we're still alive. We go on ploughin those weed fields of ours, 'n fishin fer clams, oysters 'n smelts. We still try to make ends meet 'n not to die before passin away. Mustn' croak ahead of yer time, I says to myself. 'n you gotta have yer hole in holy land to be sure 'n get yer place in Paradise. As fer the rest, we ain't got not'n else.

But whatever we got, we sure would of liked to keep it, I'm tellin you. Would of liked to stay in our houses 'n keep our lands a while longer. Ain't real lands, fer that matter, more like waste lands they says, that got no owner; so our forefathers settled there just like that, quietly 'n without makin any fuss. We was countin on stayin a few more generations without hurtin no one. Wouldn' of been high livin, we was never well off; but we could of tried to go on as before, gatherin kindlings fer winter, cuttin holes in the ice to fish fer smelts. Then, come Spring, we'd be on the look-out fer the wild geese cause they tell you the sap is just about to trickle fr'm the trees 'n yer lungs are gonna get their deep breath fer the new summer. 'n you'll watch fer the month of July with its blueberries 'n its string-beans, 'n the month of August with its corn-cobs, 'n Fall with...

...By next Fall, *la Sainte*'ll be with her boy. 'n Laurette à Johnny will also be gone. 'n Jos à Polyte, 'n l'Orignal 'n... 'n then I think it'll be our turn, me 'n Gapi. They gonna swipe all the coast-lands, they says, cause it ain't eugienic 'n it hurts the country's economy. I ain't too sure where me 'n Gapi are gonna settle down, we ain't got no boy in Montreal, 'n no kinfolk in the States. But we can't keep on stayin here, all by ourselves, 'n hurtin the country, I says to Gapi.

But Gapi, he ain't so sure we're rockin the boat. Figures, in his short life, he's seen more often people sufferin in the country, than a country bein hurt by the people. 'n he says, a land that can't support you, if they take it away fr'm you, it sure won't support any better the ones the're givin it to. That's not the way, he says, they'll be able to transplant people 'n... Well, I stop him right there, Gapi, 'n I tell him to quit complainin. Grab yer overalls 'n yer underwear, I says to him, 'n stand ready. Yep you gotta stand ready fer the next Expulsion. Cause, this time, I don't know when we'll come back. I don't know when... when we'll have a country of our own, once 'n fer all, where we'll be able to plant our string-beans, 'n to gather barrowfuls of sea-weeds to bank our houses once more... I don't know when... I don't know when...

We ain't got not'n they can cense, them censors. That's what I told'em. 'n Gapi too, told'em. We ain't got no more lands; we ain't sure of our religion; 'n we don't know our nationality. I think we ain't got one. They told us we was lucky to be still alive. That's true, all right... We're still alive... They told us that. But if we wasn', I think nobody would notice it, nobody. Not even the census. Well, if a time comes when a person can no longer name his religion, his race, his country, his land, 'n when he can no longer name the language he's speakin, well, maybe that person no longer knows what kind of a person he really is. Maybe he don't know not'n any more.

But me, I'll tell the gov'ment: I don't know not'n, I don't got not'n, I may be not'n either. But I'm still alive, ain't I. 'n right now, I believe my name is still *la Sagouine*. With a name like that, they can't mix me up with'em censors or with the doctor's missus. So they'll just have to reco'nize me when I'll be by their side, walkin down the Queen's Highway.

XVI

_____ DEATH

I live down by the wharf, but it ain't there I was born. A lot higher, 'fore the war. The other war, the first one. They says it wasn' the first one, many more, they was, 'fore that one. I can believe it, but I didn' know it. Two of them, I knew about; that's enough to have an idea. A small one. I'd take another drop of tea, if you don't mind.

They call me *la Sagouine*, yep! 'n come to think of it, if my mother was still alive, I think she wouldn' be able to remember my Christian name, not even her. 'n yet, I got one. Baptize me, they did, as sure as I'm here. Even had som'one special to carry me, better believe it, 'n a godmother, 'n a godfather. They was all people fr'm aroun' home, my father use' to tell. Baptized at home, baptized in church 'n swaddled. Went through the whole ceremony 'fore I had my eyes open. Which goes to say we're all the same at that age. It's later that... You better drink yer tea while it's hot. It'll wash yer stomach 'n yer kidneys. Me, that's where I feel the weakest. At night, I got pain like you wouldn' believe. Right down here by my spine. It's like my kidneys was all twisted, 'n every night the Good Lord brings, they start unwindin like a spring.

Maybe it ain't Him at all that brings'em nights, 'n the pain... When Gapi talks like that, I make'm shut up. You can't talk like that, I says to him. The Good Lord knows His business. ...Gapi, he figures it ain't fair. Says that if the Good Lord was that good, He wouldn' let the poor folks suffer fer no reason. But I make'm shut up. Now, we ain't gonna start blasphemin, fer Chrissake! 'n if some evil comes to us, it's cause we done some. Fair enough... Gapi, he figures the bad things people does, they ain't real bad, more like playin little tricks on the Good Lord, fer the fun of it. 'n the Good Lord don't need to get so worked up about it 'n treat us like we was mean folks tryin to act bad jus' to be bad.

...At night, grabs me right here, it does, in the belly 'n down my spine. Twice I went to town to see the doctor, but.. couldn' make up my mind. Laurette à Johnny spread aroun' that, once in town, I don't see the doctor cause I got som'n else to do there besides runnin around hospitals. She can sure talk, Laurette. After Johnny passed away, she curled up her hair 'n started playin widow. Shameless, she is. 'n it'd started even before that. Like they says, a cover fer each pot; but some folks got a lotta pots... Heh!... Can't make up my mind yet. Once the doctor pr'nounces 'mself, he pr'nounces 'mself, 'n you're stuck with the sickness he came up with. It ain't really that I'm afraid of bein sick... What I'm afraid of, is a sickness that's got no cure.

...When you're dead, it's fer a long while. Some folks is afraid of death. Not me. A little pain, I figure, 'n it's over. Suffered enough in my life so as to be able to take a bit more. Ain't death that troubles me, it's what comes after... Is it really true what they says in their big picture catechism? Pewgatory, limbo, hell... Gapi, he says like this, that if the Good Lord is good... But I make'm shut up... He says, they can't be no hell fer the poor folks, cause their hell, they got it right here.

...When we got married, first we went to see the priest 'n ask' him to perform the ceremony. But he refused, cause we was family. *Can't do it*, he says, *cause you're close-related*. True, we was a little of the same kin: my late mother 'n his father, well, they was brother 'n sister. So he says: *'cordin to the law that rules wedd'ns, I can't join first cousins*. So Gapi looks at me, 'n I looks at him, 'n he says: *If it's okay with you, we'll go 'n get married at the minister's*. We found the minister that didn' make no fuss at all, 'n we got out of there man 'n wife. Two weeks later, I can remember, Gapi was comin home fr'm his oysterin 'n I was goin to meet'm at the wharf, when we ran across Father Nap: he was a priest at Sainte-Marie's in'em days, 'n he told us:

Listen, you two, you know you ain't married. If you came with me, maybe I could fix that.

So Gapi looks at me 'n I looks at him, 'n he says:

If we was kin last week, we're still kin today; ain't no need fer yer wedd'ns.

But Father Nap didn' blow his top; he says:

Won't be long, come with me to the sacristy 'n I'll marry you in church, it'll be done real fast.

Gapi looks at me 'n I looks at him:

If it's okay with you, he says...

So we followed Father Nap to the sacristy. He confessed us, married us 'n blessed us; he even refused the buck Gapi wanned to give him. Like Gapi says: *with all of this, we'been married twice, mus' be worth som'n*. A real weddin it was, I even had a weddin ring. A nice big weddin ring of pure limitation gold. I lost it on the church steps, I remember. But, like they says: when you'had twelve children, you can always lose yer weddin ring...

...Yep, twelve children. 'n I managed to save three. Nine of them died when they was babies. You see, in 'em motherin days, they wasn' even bankin fer the houses, 'n only green wood 'n kindlins fer heatin. 'n to make things worse, them nine was born between All Saints' day 'n the Spring thaw. The three that was born with the raspberry pickin, survived. Of course, it's yer mother that delivered'm. A saint, yer mother is, a real kind woman, yep, 'n right now, ain't no doubt she's in heaven. She use' to supply everythin, yer mother did: the diapers, the blankets, the wrappin clothes 'n even the hot water. A real kind woman. If they had been more people like her, maybe I could of saved the nine others. Ah! well, like I says to Gapi, fer them at least, I ain't got no worry: the're all together in a bunch at the cemetery. Ain't got no worry. Them, I know the're okay; they sure didn' have time to be bad. 'n I had just enough time of baptizin'em all.

I go to town every time I get my check fr'm the gov'ment. But they won't catch me again in'em houses. I take the long way around not to pass in front of them. La Rosie called me over the other day, but I didn' show her I'd heard, 'n then I shouted back that she was goin straight to hell. Come on over, she tells me, I gotta talk to you. I says: you got any men in there? I'm all by myself, she says. All right, I answered, I'll go 'n see. Heh!... Don't make no sense livin like that at her age, with death written all over her face. It's just like I says to the judge: made a promise to Sainte-Anne, I did, 'n

I'll keep it. 'n now, me 'n the judge, we're like brother 'n sister.

...Thanks. Sure would like to make good tea like that. Coats yer lungs, it does... Good tea leaves, that's fer sure, good tea leaves. A person can almost see his whole life in there. I'll end up goin to see the doctor. 'n as long as I'm goin, might as well see the best one. A specialist of the belly. That's where the trouble is. The biggest trouble always comes fr'm there. Comin to life or passin away. 'n in between, it ain't long. Take it fr'm *la Sagouine*. Seems like it was yesterday. We was by the moor, pickin blueberries, 'n my grandmother use' to say:

Pick only the blueberries that are real ripe. The other ones are good fer seeds. All that's white, you musn' touch it.

'n I was sayin to myself: all that's white, you musn' touch it. That's why we was wearin a white First Communion veil. We was all young 'n it made us think. Later, you forget, you think of not'n. You just try to make ends meet 'n patch up yer life so it won't show too much. But when you tore yer skirt once, after that it always shows. So, it's better not to think about it no more. You figure you'll be able to stop thinkin. But it's too much. There's the dances, the home-made beer, the children you didn' get a chance to save, the bickerin with the neighbours, the baloney on Friday, 'n then the Sunday mass that you avoid cause yer hat was too worn out to put on yer head, 'n you didn' wanna be laughed at. It's just too much fer a whole lifetime. The Good Lord may be good, but...

The priest tells us he forgives everythin, cause he's infinitively good. Well, provided you feel sorry.

That's fair. II told it to Gapi. If you wanna have yer sins forgiven, you gotta be sorry 'n firmly resolve not to do it again... Now, does that mean that if you had to start all over again...? Yep, if you had to start all over, you'd have to change yer way of livin, that's all.

...Ain't easy. Cause a person don't always have a choice. If my children had been short of not'n, like the other folks' kids, wouldn'of had to exile myself to the city, on Main street, or to be on the look-out fer steamers fr'm the ol' countries. Wouldn' of had to. *Well, you didn' have to hide fr'm me what you did with Dan's boy, down by the moor of Saint-Norbert,* Gapi says to me. *You could have tol'me 'fore I married you,* he says. Yep, could of told him, fer sure. But I didn' have time, cause it happened with him like it happened with Dan's boy 'n I didn' have time. 'n then, why tell him, anyway? Would of hurt him, 'n it was too late. Even if you're sorry... when you did it, you did it.

To do well, a person would have to be sorry ahead of time. Well, that ain't easy. I says like this, the biggest sins are the ones you do, knowin it ain't right, but doin it anyway. 'n bein free to make yer choice. Ah! I know a person 's always free, sure, but... but is he always free?

Take *la Bessoune* that went crazy over a secret love 'n, they says, she never let herself talk to nobody about it... she couldn' help it, 'n so it looks like she wasn' free. Some says it was the devil, 'n others says it was the priest. Anyway, the poor gal never got out of it 'n the Good Lord must of had mercy on her, cause she died with her medals around her neck.

...Sometimes it ain't easy to be sorry. You can try all you want, 'n quarrel with yerself, 'n make yerself listen to reason, 'n bang yer head with yer firm resolution, you just won't get it in yer heart. Sometimes a person ain't free to be sorry.

...Around night time, when the sea turns a different shade, 'n when the seagulls start with their harsh cries around the wharf, sometimes I take a walk on the bridge, 'n I wait. I wait to see if one of the steamers that was lost durin the war, the last one, wouldn' appear again in the far distance, with all its men on board. 'n I remember the song he use' to sing, sittin on the bow, all alone, far fr'm the others. He had straw hair 'n big sad eyes, that one. If the war hadn' grab'd him, 'n if he'd asked me to go with him, far away, in'em strange lands, far fr'm Gapi, 'n fr'm my children, 'n... he didn' ask me, 'n I stayed here. So, can a person know ahead of time what he'd do, if he had to do it over again?... You never have the chance to do it over, anyway. So I really don't see why you gotta turn yerself inside out to come up with a firm resolution.

...Especially when we're not too sure if it's gonna be useful.

If only we could know. Know before reachin the other side. Cause once there, it'll be too late. What we done, we done. If there's not'n on the other side, wouldn' have to worry about every little thing. We could live the life we got. Wouldn' be a hell of a lot, but we'd live it without havin our guts blamin us fer it. 'n if there is som'n, what do you think it could be? Is it the hell possible we'd have to start sufferin there too? Didn' we have enough? Are we gonna have to freeze our feet again, fr'm the beginnin of Advent to the end of Lent; eat warmed-up baked beans fr'm Sunday to Sunday; sell clams, quahaugs 'n mussels fr'm gate to gate; wear the ol' clothes the doctor's missus gives away outta charity; 'n bury our children 'fore they even had a chance to open their eyes; 'n all of that lastin fer as long as the Good Lord's eternity?... Is it the hell possible?

...Yet, we wasn' askin fer much. We ain't even asked to be born, none of us, better believe it! 'n we don't ask to die either. So then, they gonna give us another life on the other side that's gonna look like this one? But, that one, we can't turn it down, we can't get us outta that one. Gapi, he says we can always jump off the wharf when we had our fill of this rotten life. But, is there gonna be a wharf on the other side?

I think I'll end up goin to see the doctor...

...All I'm askin is to have a little peace of mind up there. 'n I'll do no wrong, that's fer sure. Anyway, there comes a time when a person no longer has the feelin or the guts to do wrong. If they want me to go to mass 'n to them sacraments, I'll be there. Even at Vespers, durin all their eternity that'll last eternally. I'll do anythin they tell me. I'll resist temptation 'n I'll be heartily sorry fer havin offended thee. 'n let it be over. No more cold winters, no more baked beans, no more pain in yer gut, let it be over.

Course, if there's som'n more, we ain't gonna be fussy. Ain't use' to fancy things. Ain't askin fer castles, or Californias, or plastic flowers. But if the angels could whip up a wild-duck stew 'n a store-bought coconut pie, 'n if our Father-in-Heaven in person could come around 'n call the dance on Saturday nights, we wouldn' mind it. Fer a Paradise like that one, we wouldn' whine so much about death... wouldn' be afraid any more... we'd croak happy, My God, yes!...

...First thing tomorrow, I'll go see the doctor.

THE END